Dragon Slayers' Academy 3

CLASS TRIP to the
CAVE of DOOM

For Jeff Hall
—K.H. McM.

For my dearest Marie
—B.B.

Dragon Slayers' Academy™ 3

CLASS TRIP to the CAVE of DOOM

By K.H. McMullan

Illustrated by Bill Basso

GROSSET & DUNLAP • NEW YORK

Library of Congress Cataloging-in-Publication Data

McMullan, K.H.
  Class trip to the cave of doom / by K.H. McMullan ; illustrated by Bill Basso.
    p. cm. — (Dragon Slayers' Academy 3)
  Summary: Wiglaf joins the other students of Dragon Slayers' Academy in searching the Dark Forest for the Cave of Doom, which supposedly contains the gold of the dead dragon Seetha.
  [1. Dragons—Fiction. 2. Buried treasure—Fiction. 3. Caves—Fiction. 4. Schools—Fiction.] I. Basso, Bill, ill. II. Title. III. Series: McMullan, K.H. Dragon Slayers' Academy 3.
PZ7.M4789cl 1998   98-35524
[Fic]—dc21   CIP
                                                    AC

ISBN 0-448-42290-5   A B C D E F G H I J

Chapter 1

link! Clink! Clink! Mordred, the headmaster of Dragon Slayers' Academy, banged his spoon on his glass. *Clink! Clink! Clink!*

"Boys!" Mordred's loud voice filled the DSA dining hall. "I have a surprise for you!"

Egad! thought Wiglaf. *What now?* Mordred's last surprise had been a scrubbing party. Wiglaf had been up half the night, working on the stew pot.

"Maybe Uncle Mordred caught the boys who threw his boots into the moat," Angus whispered to Wiglaf. Angus was the headmaster's nephew. But Wiglaf didn't hold that against him. "Or maybe," Angus went on, "he found out who dropped Sir Mort's false teeth into the cider jug."

"Shh, Angus!" said Erica, who was also Wiglaf's friend. "We're supposed to be—"

"QUIIIIIIET!" Mordred roared.

A hush fell over the dining hall.

"That's better." The headmaster smiled. His gold tooth shone in the torchlight. "Now, as you know, Wiglaf has killed two dragons."

Wiglaf gasped. Could it be? Was Mordred at last going to honor him as a hero?

"But tell me, boys," Mordred continued. "Did Wiglaf bring back any dragon gold for *me?*"

"Nooooooo!" the DSA students cried.

Wiglaf slid down in his seat. He should have known! Mordred was only picking on him—again.

Wiglaf was sick of being picked on. Back home, his twelve brothers picked on him all the time. They called him Runt, because he was small for his age. They made fun of his carrot-colored hair and his pet pig, Daisy. They teased him about his tender-hearted ways.

Wiglaf had hoped that things would be better at school. He had come to DSA to learn to be a hero. And he *had* killed two dragons. A young one named Gorzil and his mother, Seetha. But the truth was, Wiglaf had killed them by accident. He could never have cut off their heads. Or poked his sword into their guts. The very thought of blood made Wiglaf sick to his stomach. Still, he *had* killed them. That should count for something. And he was the only boy at DSA ever to kill *any* dragon. But Mordred didn't care about dead dragons. All he cared about was getting his hands on their gold.

"Wiglaf brought me no gold," Mordred moaned softly. "No gold." Then his violet eyes lit up. "But rumors are flying!" he exclaimed. "Villagers in Ratswhiskers say that before Seetha died, she hid all her gold in a cave in the Dark Forest."

Erica jumped up. "Let *me* go to that cave, sir!" she cried. "I shall bring you Seetha's gold!"

Wiglaf smiled. Erica was so gung ho about dragon slaying. Mordred did not let girls into his school. So Erica cut her straight brown hair and dressed as a boy so she could go to DSA. Everyone there called her Eric. Only Wiglaf knew that she was really Erica. Princess Erica, as a matter of fact.

"You *shall* go, Eric," Mordred roared. "*All* of you are going on a class trip to the Dark Forest! That is my surprise! All of you are going to hunt for Seetha's gold!"

"Hooray!" Erica cried.

A few others cheered. But not Wiglaf. The

Dark Forest was not exactly a vacation spot. It was *dark*, for one thing. And very scary.

"You shall meet in the castle yard tomorrow morning," Mordred continued. "Then you shall march into the Dark Forest. And the boy who finds Seetha's gold..." Mordred rubbed his hands together. "...will get a great big *prize!*"

"Hooray!" everyone cheered this time.

"Wiggie!" Erica called over the cheering. "I am sure to find Seetha's gold, so you and Angus stick with me. That way, you can share the prize!"

Wiglaf nodded. If only the prize were some of Seetha's gold. Then he could pay the seven pennies he still owed DSA for his tuition. He could send some money to his greedy family back in Pinwick. And maybe—just maybe—if he found Seetha's gold, Mordred would stop picking on him.

Chapter 2

"Jump, boys! Higher!" Coach Plungett, the DSA slaying teacher, called early the next morning. His brown pageboy wig blew in the breeze as he counted jumping jacks. "Ninety-one! Ninety-two! Exercise will make you manly men, like me!"

Wiglaf had never done so many jumping jacks. His arms were ready to drop off.

But Coach kept counting. "One hundred three!" he cried. "Jumping is a manly way to warm up on a chilly morning!"

The boys had stumbled into the castle yard

before sunup. Coach Plungett put them into groups. Coach was the leader of the Bloodhounds. Wiglaf was a Bloodhound. Angus and Erica were Bloodhounds, too. So were the big Marley brothers: Barley, Charlie, Farley, and Harley.

Wiglaf looked over at the Marleys doing sloppy jumping jacks. He couldn't tell one brother from another. They never said much. They were known for playing jokes. Wiglaf was pretty sure the Marleys had thrown Mordred's boots into the moat.

"One hundred twenty!" Coach counted.

"I cannot...do any...more!" Wiglaf gasped.

"This is nothing," yelled Erica. She was jumping next to him. "I once did six hundred jumping jacks. And I wasn't even out of breath."

Wiglaf could barely hear what Erica was saying. Her tool belt was clanking too loudly.

She had sent away for it from the Sir Lancelot Fan Club catalog. All sorts of fine dragon-slaying equipment hung from the wide silver belt. A canteen. A collapsible goblet. A spyglass. A magnifying glass. A rope. A small copy of *The Sir Lancelot Handbook*. A mini-torch. A pack of dry sticks for starting fires. A spare sword. A lice comb. And a toothpick.

All Wiglaf had was a beat-up sword. His lucky rag was tied to the handle. But now, as he did his one hundred eighty-second jumping jack, he was just as glad not to be wearing a heavy tool belt.

"Where is Mordred anyway?" Erica asked.

"You know Uncle Mordred hates to get up before noon," Angus answered.

Angus moved his arms up and down as Coach counted. But he kept his feet planted on the ground. Since Angus was Mordred's nephew, Coach Plungett pretended not to notice.

"Two hundred!" Coach called. "Halt!"

Wiglaf stopped jumping. He thought *halt* was the most beautiful word he'd ever heard.

"Now hit the ground for two hundred push-ups!" Coach called.

Wiglaf groaned. Was Coach trying to slay them?

Luckily, at that moment, the castle door opened. Mordred stepped outside. He raised a megaphone to his mouth. He called, "Atten*tion!*"

The boys snapped up straight and tall.

"Each group leader has a map of part of the Dark Forest," Mordred went on. "Each map shows all the caves in that part. Look in every cave, boys. There's gold in one of them!"

"The Bloodhounds shall find it!" Erica cried.

"Nay!" a boy called out. "The Bulldogs!"

"No! The Wolfhounds!" called another boy.

"Wrong!" another piped up. "The Poodles!"

"That's the spirit, boys!" Mordred cried. He walked down the castle steps. Six skinny DSA student teachers hurried over to him. They carried a large thronelike chair with poles attached to its seat. The student teachers lowered the chair. Mordred sat down in it.

"They're going to *carry* him?" Wiglaf exclaimed.

"You didn't think Uncle Mordred would walk to the Dark Forest, did you?" Angus asked.

"No monkeying around," Mordred called. "I'll come check on you from my camp." He gave a signal. Four student teachers picked up his chair. The others picked up his camping gear. Wiglaf saw that it included pillows, thick blankets, and red pajamas with feet.

Tweeeeeeeeeeeeeeeeeet! Mordred gave a blast on his silver whistle. They were off!

Coach led the Bloodhounds across the castle yard. Everyone carried a heavy pack. The

big Marley brothers carried theirs with ease. Wiglaf staggered under his as he marched over the DSA drawbridge.

Wiglaf looked down into the castle moat. How well he remembered Seetha splashing in its waters before she went down for the last time. The secret of where she hid her dragon gold had gone down with her. Now, he was off to hunt for that gold. And, by St. George, he was going to find it!

The Bloodhounds marched up Huntsman's Path. They marched through Vulture Valley. They marched around Leech Lake. And across Swamp River Ridge.

"Halt!" Coach ordered at last.

Wiglaf stopped. There was that lovely word *halt* again. He gladly dropped his pack to the ground.

Coach took out his map. He looked at it for a long time. "We are now in the south part of the Dark Forest," he said. Then he frowned.

He turned the map upside down. "Or are we in the north part?"

Wiglaf and Angus looked over Coach's shoulder.

"Zounds!" Wiglaf cried. "There must be a hundred caves on that map!"

"We'll be marching around here forever!" Angus said. "Let's give up and go home."

"Bloodhounds never give up!" Erica cried.

"That's the way, Eric!" Coach said. "All right, Bloodhounds. On your feet."

The Bloodhounds picked up their packs. They started off. The Marleys marched behind Wiglaf. They began a contest to see which one of them could burp the loudest. Wiglaf thought they all should get first prize.

"Coach?" Erica called out. "I made up a Bloodhound marching song."

"Good work!" Coach cried. "Why don't we sing it as we march?"

Erica sang her song through once. Then all

the Bloodhounds marched through the Dark Forest, singing:

> *"We're the mighty Bloodhounds!*
> *We're dogged and we're bold!*
> *We're the mighty Bloodhounds!*
> *We'll track down Seetha's gold!*
> *We'll put our noses to the ground!*
> *We'll give a mighty sniff!*
> *Will we ever loose the scent?*
> *No! No! Not us! As if!*
> *'Cause...we're the mighty Bloodhounds!*
> *Hear us when we yell!*
> *We're the mighty Bloodhounds!*
> *And do we ever smell!"*

The Bloodhounds looked in twelve caves that morning. Most were empty. But not all. The Cave of Really-Loud-Snoring housed a family of sleeping bears. Cave Hole-in-the-Roof was full of puddles. And Jolly-Good-

Times Cave was piled high with old mead flasks.

Inside Jolly-Good-Times Cave, the Marleys started yelling and whooping and picking up the flasks. They shook them upside down over their mouths. They were hoping for a drop or two of mead, but the flasks were empty

"Charlie!" cried Coach. "Parley! Whatever your names are! Cut that out!"

He lined everyone up again. Off they marched down Snakes' Path.

"Say, my manly men!" Coach called as they marched. "Who is going to find the gold?"

"The Bloodhounds!" Erica yelled.

Wiglaf hoped Erica was right. That would make all his pain worthwhile. The heavy pack hurt his back. He had blisters on every toe. He was hungry. And it wasn't easy keeping up with Erica.

At a bend in the road, Wiglaf heard a low growl.

"Is that your stomach?" he asked Erica.

"No," she said. "I thought it was yours."

The growling grew louder.

Suddenly a wild man leaped out at them! He had thick white hair. His beard hung down to his knees. He swung a pointed stick over his head and charged at the Bloodhounds!

Chapter 3

Wiglaf ran behind a tree for cover. The Marleys hid behind a big rock. Angus hid behind Wiglaf.

Erica stood her ground beside Coach.

The wild man shook his stick. "Danger!" he cried. "Do not go to the Cave of Doom!"

"Doom?" Wiglaf whispered. "Did he say *doom?*"

"I think so," Angus whispered back. "I'm not going into any cave called Doom."

"Danger!" the hermit cried again. "Do not pass go! Do not stick rocks up your nose!"

"Be gone!" Coach called with a toss of his

head, which made his wig slide to the left.

"First hear my tale!" the hermit cried. "It's a sad tale. Nothing like a fish tail. More like a pig tail. Kind of twisty..."

"Get on with it!" Coach ordered.

"Seven brave men followed me into the Cave of Doom," the hermit said. "We were looking for Seetha's gold!"

"Seetha?" Wiglaf cried. "The dragon?"

"No, Seetha the chipmunk!" The hermit glared at Wiglaf. "Yes, Seetha the dragon. Now, seven men followed me in. But I alone came out alive. Alive, yes. But nutty as a fruitcake. That's why they call me Crazy Looey!"

Wiglaf hoped Looey wasn't both crazy and dangerous. He felt for his lucky rag.

"Oh, we read Seetha's warning," Crazy Looey went on. "But still I led my men deep into the cave. On the cave floor we saw a gold coin. I picked it up. And before you could say, 'The eensy, weensy spider went up the water spout...' " Crazy Looey started making little spider-climbing movements with his fingers.

"Go on, man!" Coach cried. "Go on!"

"Before you could say that," Crazy Looey said, "the cave filled with smoke. Poison smoke! I had set off a booby trap! My seven brave men dropped in their tracks. Dead as ducks. Deader, some of them. Me? I ran. Ran so fast, my hat fell off. It was my best hat, too. The one with a turkey feather—"

"Stop!" Erica called out. "I don't believe a word of this silly story!"

Wiglaf wasn't so sure. True, there was no Cave of Doom on Coach's map. But it sounded like a place Seetha would hide her gold.

"A red-and-white striped turkey feather," Crazy Looey went on. "The prettiest darn feather you ever did see."

"Enough, Cuckoo Looey!" Coach Plungett cried. "Let us pass!"

"That's *Crazy* Looey," the hermit said. "And

I won't let you pass! No way. Not a chance. Never!"

Coach Plungett drew his sword.

"Ah ha!" said Crazy Looey as the tip of Coach's sword touched the tip of his nose. "I see your point!"

The hermit did a little dance. Then he ran away down Snakes' Path, singing: "Down came the rain and washed the spider out...."

The Bloodhounds watched until he disappeared.

Coach put away his sword. "Shame on you for hiding, Bloodhounds!" he said. "You must face danger! Be manly men, like me!"

"Coach?" said Angus. "I don't want to die in the Cave of Doom! I want to go home to DSA! We could make it by sundown."

"Angus, you know Bloodhounds never turn back," Coach scolded. "Now, let's march!"

Wiglaf picked up his pack and started marching. He thought about what Crazy

Looey had said. He didn't mind poking about in caves with old mead flasks. Or even bears, so long as they were asleep. But the Cave of Doom sounded like a very different sort of cave. Wiglaf hoped Crazy Looey had made the whole thing up.

On they marched down Snakes' Path. They passed a large rock. It was shaped like a cow.

The Marley brothers began yelling, "Moo! Moo!"

Erica stopped marching. "Look!" she cried, pointing down at her feet.

Wiglaf looked. Spread across the path in front of him was a giant footprint.

"Is th-that a dragon print?" Angus asked.

"I think so," Erica said. "But we must be sure." She took *The Sir Lancelot Handbook* from her tool belt. She handed it to Wiglaf. "Read me Chapter Two: Are You Sure It's a Dragon Print?"

Wiglaf turned the tiny pages of the book.

At last he found the spot.

"Dragon prints are big," he read. *"Very big."*

Erica dropped to her knees. She looked at the print through her magnifying glass.

"Yes!" she cried. "This print is very big."

"A dragon foot has three large toes," Wiglaf read. *"So does a dragon print."*

"One, two, three!" Erica counted. "Yes!"

"At the tip of each toe will be a deep hole made by a dragon claw," he read.

Erica brought her magnifying glass to the tip of the first toe. "Yes!" she cried. She jumped to her feet. "This is a dragon print!"

"Let's get out of here!" Angus howled.

Had this print been made by Seetha? Wiglaf wondered.

Erica called, "Coach! Come here! Quick!"

Coach Plungett hurried back to the spot.

"Egad!" he said when he saw the footprint.

"It's definitely a dragon print, sir," Erica told him.

"And look!" Wiglaf cried. He pointed to the side of the path. "There's another print! And another! They lead into the forest!"

"Put your noses to the ground, Blood-hounds!" cried Coach Plungett. "We shall follow these prints. For as sure as I'm a manly man, they were made by Seetha. And surely they shall lead us to her gold!"

Coach Plungett followed the giant footprints through the Dark Forest. The Blood-hounds followed Coach Plungett.

Wiglaf tried to keep up. But it wasn't easy. Branches scratched his face. Thorns tore at his breeches. He had too many blisters to count. And the Marleys were burping again.

Angus turned around. "Here," he said. He handed Wiglaf a stick of his Wild Boar jerky. "This always makes me feel better."

"Thanks," Wiglaf said. But it did not make him feel better. It only made him thirsty.

On the Bloodhounds marched. At last the

dragon prints led to a creek. It was wide and deep. It smelled of dead fish. Thick green ooze lay on top of the water like a blanket. It reminded Wiglaf of something. But he could not think what.

"This is either Clear Water Creek," Coach said. "Or—" he turned the map sideways, "Stinking Green Creek."

Wiglaf had a pretty good idea which creek this was. And now he knew what it reminded him of—his mother's cabbage soup!

Erica took the spyglass from her tool belt. She held it to her eye. "I see dragon prints on the far side of the creek," she told Coach.

"Then we must wade across it," Coach said.

"No!" Angus cried. "Not across *that!*"

The Marleys began to grumble.

"There is no bridge," Coach pointed out. "Wading is the only way. Stop being such babies," he added. "What's a little stinking green ooze to manly men? Now follow me!"

"Sir?" Erica said. "There is another way." Erica took the rope from her tool belt. She threw one end over a tree branch that hung above the creek. Next, she made a loop. She pulled it tight around the branch. Then she knotted the end of the rope.

"Tah dah!" Erica cried. "We can swing across!"

Wiglaf grinned. Back home, he had swung across Pinwick Creek hundreds of times.

"I'll go first," Erica said. She backed up. Her tool belt jangled as she ran for the rope. She jumped on the knot. She swung easily across the creek and hopped off on the far bank.

"Well done!" cried Coach Plungett.

Erica beamed. "Who's next?" she called. She threw the rope over to the other side. Coach caught it. He swung across.

Charlie Marley went next. Then Barley. Then Farley. Harley burped as he swung over.

Harley threw Angus the rope. "Alas, Wiglaf!" Angus whispered. "I'm scared!"

"You can do it," Wiglaf said.

Angus made a few false starts. Then he stood on the knot. Wiglaf pulled the rope back. He gave Angus a mighty push.

Angus sailed over the creek. He landed on the far bank. "Easy as pie!" he exclaimed.

Angus threw Wiglaf the rope. Wiglaf caught it. He backed up. He began to run. He jumped and swung out over the creek.

It was just like swinging over Pinwick Creek—except for one thing. Back home, he never had a great big heavy pack on his back.

Wiglaf felt his fingers slip down the rope.

He lost his hold!

The next thing Wiglaf knew, he was falling toward the slimy green water.

Chapter 4

"Yiiiiiiiiiiiiiiiiii!" Wiglaf screamed. He splashed down into Stinking Green Creek.

Stinking was right! The water smelled *exactly* like his mother's cabbage soup. Slimy green ooze trickled into Wiglaf's eyes. And his ears. And his mouth. Yuck!

On the bank, the Marleys roared with laughter.

"Wiggie!" Erica called. "Are you all right?"

"Don't swallow!" Angus yelled. "That water will kill you!"

Wiglaf spit out as much ooze as he could.

Coach held out a long tree branch. Wiglaf

took hold of it. He struggled toward the shore. At last he waded out of the water. He was stinking, green, and oozy.

The Marleys were laughing their heads off.

"Cut it out!" Erica growled at them. "It's not funny." She looked at Wiglaf. She put a hand to her mouth to keep from laughing. "Well, maybe it is. A little."

Angus couldn't help smiling, too.

Great, Wiglaf thought. *Now even my friends are laughing at me!* How he wished this class trip was over.

Wiglaf untied his lucky rag from his sword. He wrung it out. With it he wiped the green slime from his face and arms. He dried his hair. He patted off his clothes.

Coach slapped Wiglaf on the back. "Up and at 'em, now. That's the way. Are you ready to hit the road like a manly man?"

Wiglaf nodded. "Ready," he said. He was

sticky and wet. But he wasn't a quitter. He still wanted to find Seetha's gold.

"Take the lead, Eric," Coach said.

Erica grinned. "Let's march!" she called.

The Bloodhounds marched. They followed the prints onto a road. It was the very road Wiglaf had taken from his home in Pinwick to DSA. Soon the prints led back into the forest again. The afternoon sun dipped low in the sky. And still they followed the dragon prints.

Suddenly Erica stopped. "Coach!" she cried.

"Keep going, Eric," Coach said. "I see more prints over there."

"But we have seen them before!" Erica said. "We are back on Snakes' Path! See? The prints led us in a circle!"

"No jokes!" Angus cried. "I beg of you!"

"Upon my honor, I am not joking," Erica said. "Over there is the rock that looks like a cow. And here is the first print we found!"

Wiglaf saw that Erica was right. "Oh, flea bites!" he cried.

"Alas and alack!" Angus said sadly.

Only the Marleys didn't care. They'd found an anthill and were poking it with sticks.

"How did we *do* that?" Coach said. He took out the map again. He turned it this way and that. Then he pushed back his wig and scratched his hairless head for a long time.

Wiglaf staggered over to the cow-shaped rock. He leaned against it. He felt like crying. He was cold. His feet hurt. He smelled like dead fish. And all for nothing!

Wiglaf slid down against the rock. Then he noticed strange scratch marks on it. He squinted at the rock in the fading light. And he saw that the scratch marks were letters!

"Coach!" Wiglaf cried. "Over here! Hurry!"

Coach Plungett and the other Bloodhounds ran over. Erica lit her mini-torch. Scratched onto the rock by a dragon's claw was:

YOU FOLLOWED MY PRINTS
AND NOW—SURPRISE!
ALL YOU GOT WAS EXERCISE!
YOU'LL NEVER TRACK DOWN
MY HIDING SPOT!
FOR DRAGONS CAN FLY—
AND YOU CANNOT!
S E E T H A v o n F L A M B É
P.S. TURN BACK NOW!

"I say we take Seetha's advice!" Angus cried. "Let's turn back *now!*"

"Never!" Erica growled. "Seetha planned to lead us on this wild goose chase before she died. But her mean trick only makes me want to find her gold all the more!"

Wiglaf kicked at the cow-shaped rock. How he wished the Bloodhounds could turn back— just this once.

But Coach had other ideas.

"We shall camp here," he said. "The ground is hard and rocky. But manly men can sleep anywhere!"

The Bloodhounds got out their sleeping bags. Coach began setting up his tent.

In a low voice, Harley Marley called out, "Coach?"

Wiglaf stared. He had heard the Marleys burp. He had heard them laugh and whoop and moo like cows. But this was the first time he had heard any of them speak.

"Yes?" Coach answered. "What is it?"

"We'll set up your tent for you," Harley said. The other Marleys nodded.

Harley and Farley unfolded Coach's tent. Charlie and Barley pounded the tent poles into the ground. Wiglaf and Angus watched, wide-eyed.

At last camp was set up. The Bloodhounds made a fire. Coach passed out sandwiches.

"What *is* this?" Angus asked when he got his. "Hard bread and moldy cheese?"

Coach took a look. "No, you got the *moldy* bread and *hard* cheese sandwich."

Wiglaf pulled his wet sleeping bag close to the fire. He hoped it would dry. Then he stuck his sandwich on a stick. He toasted it over the campfire. It didn't make it taste any better. But at least it was warm going down.

Erica poured cider into her collapsible goblet. The rest of the Bloodhounds took turns drinking from the jug. Wiglaf hoped it was not the jug that had been home to Sir Mort's false teeth.

"Into your sleeping bags, Bloodhounds," Coach said after supper. "I am going to tell you a ghost story."

Wiglaf slid into his sleeping bag. It still smelled of fish. But it was almost dry.

"Once there lived an executioner," Coach began. "Every night at twelve o'clock, he took his axe and chopped off someone's head. He always wore a black hood. So no one knew what he looked like."

"Coach!" cried Angus. "This is too scary!"

"Oh, stop up your ears, Angus," Erica snapped. "The rest of us want to hear this."

Wiglaf wasn't so sure. A story about be-heading was likely to be bloody. And Wiglaf's stomach turned over if he even thought about blood.

"The executioner," Coach continued, "walked through the Dark Forest with his axe. And as he went, he sang this song:

"If ever you hear me walking by,
*It may be **you** who's the next to die!*
I'll lay your neck on a chopping block,
And whack off your head at twelve o'clock!
I'll wrap you up in a big white sheet,
And bury you down six feet deep!
Then the worms crawl in! And the worms crawl out!

They'll eat your guts and then spit them out!
They'll peel your skin! They'll drink your blood!
Till all that's left are your bones in the mud!"

Wiglaf was about to stick his fingers in his ears. He didn't want to hear another word! But Coach went on with his tale. "The executioner chopped off hundreds and hundreds of heads. And then one day, it happened."

"What happened?" asked Erica.

"The executioner swung his axe too hard," Coach said. "And he chopped off his own bloody head!"

Uck! Wiglaf hoped he wouldn't be sick!

"The executioner's head rolled down a hill," Coach went on. "It splashed into Bottomless Lake and sank to the bottom."

"I'm glad he's dead!" Angus cried.

"Oh, he's dead, all right," Coach said. "But now his ghost walks through the Dark Forest.

He's looking for heads to chop off. For, you see, he needs a new head."

Angus began whimpering with fear.

Wiglaf held tight to his lucky rag.

"Now every night at midnight," Coach went on, "the ghost sings his song. So be careful in the Dark Forest, boys. If you hear someone singing: 'The worms crawl in, the worms crawl out...' Beware! It's the headless executioner, coming after *you!*"

Chapter 5

"**I**'m afraid to sleep," Angus whispered.

"Scaredy-cat!" Erica laughed. But Wiglaf thought that even her voice sounded shaky.

"Maybe it's not *this* Dark Forest," Angus said. "Maybe it's some *other* Dark Forest."

"Maybe," Wiglaf said. But as far as he knew there was only one Dark Forest.

Wiglaf heard a hissing sound. And another! He sat up in his sleeping bag. His heart was pounding. But it was only the Marleys. They were taking turns spitting into the campfire.

"Coach, I can't go to sleep," Angus said. "I'm afraid the ghost will come."

"Piffle!" Coach said. "I told you that story to make you brave. I want you to grow up to be a big, strong, manly man—like me!" He stood up. "I am going to my tent," he said. "Sleep well!"

"Good night, Coach!" Erica called.

"Sweet dreams!" called Harley Marley.

Then all the Marleys started laughing.

What is their problem? Wiglaf wondered.

Coach ducked into his tent. He closed the tent flap behind him. Wiglaf heard him humming a marching song as he got ready for bed.

Wiglaf closed his eyes. He heard owls calling. He heard crickets singing. He heard a Marley hocking something up from deep in his throat. He heard a horrible, bloodcurdling scream. Wiglaf's eyes popped open.

Suddenly Coach shot out of his tent. He held his sleeping bag tightly around him. He jumped around, screaming.

"The executioner's after him!" Angus cried. He disappeared into his sleeping bag.

"Help!" Coach screamed. "Don't let them get me!"

The Marleys rolled on the ground, laughing.

Coach kept jumping around. Then—*BONK!* He hit his head on a low tree branch. His nightcap and his wig stuck on the branch. But the rest of him fell to the ground.

Wiglaf jumped up. He forgot his own fear as he ran to his fallen leader.

"Coach?" Wiglaf cried. "Can you hear me?"

Coach didn't answer. He was out cold.

Erica reached Coach next. She patted his face. "Wake up, Coach!" she said.

The Marleys kept laughing and snorting.

At last Angus crawled out of his sleeping bag. He made his way slowly over to Coach. He poked him with his toe.

But Coach didn't move. Not even when

Wiglaf put his wig back on his head.

"What could have undone him so?" Erica asked. As if in answer, a sound came from inside Coach's tent: *ribbit! ribbit!*

Wiglaf and the others saw a dozen little frogs hop out of the tent. *Ribbit!* they croaked as they hopped away.

The Marleys laughed even harder.

Suddenly Wiglaf understood. No wonder the Marleys had been so helpful. They had planted the frogs inside Coach's tent!

"For a manly man," Angus said, "Coach sure is scared of frogs."

Erica splashed Coach with cold water from her canteen. At last Coach opened his eyes. He sat up. He smiled a strange smile.

"Hallo!" he said. "And who are you, young lads?"

"The Bloodhounds," Erica answered.

"You don't look like doggies!" Coach giggled.

"Uh-oh," said Angus.

"Coach?" Erica said. "Do you know your name?"

The silly smile appeared on Coach's face once more. "Is it...Rumpelstiltskin?"

"Guess again," Erica said.

"I know!" Coach exclaimed. "I'm Queen Mary!"

"He needs help," Erica said. "But nothing on my tool belt is going to do the trick."

"We have to get him to DSA," Wiglaf said.

"I'll take him!" Angus cried. He jumped up. "I'll do anything to get out of this forest!"

But Harley spoke up. "We'll take him," he said. His brothers nodded.

Wiglaf didn't think this was a very good idea. But he was not about to argue with the four big brothers.

Barley and Charlie held onto each other's arms, making a seat. Coach wobbled over and sat down on it. The Marleys lifted him up.

And they started off for DSA.

"Farewell from the queen!" Coach called. He blew kisses. Then he began to sing. "Queen Mary had a little lamb! Little lamb! Little lamb! Queen Mary had a little lamb! Its fleece was white as cheese!"

"All right, Bloodhounds!" Erica said to the two who were left. "It's just us now. We must find Seetha's gold for good old Coach Plungett! We shall make him proud of us. Because who is the best?"

"Who?" asked Angus.

"The Bloodhounds!" Erica cried.

The three of them pulled their sleeping bags into Coach's tent. They lined them up close together and crawled inside.

Wiglaf untied his lucky rag from his sword. He held it tightly and closed his eyes. He tried counting unicorns. After some two hundred, he finally fell asleep.

In the middle of the night, Wiglaf sat up

with a start. What had woken him? He listened. He heard a strange high voice, singing.

The little hairs on the back of Wiglaf's neck stood up. He squeezed his lucky rag. *Don't let it be the executioner's ghost!* he said over and over to himself.

The singing grew louder. The singer was coming closer!

"Does anybody hear singing?" Wiglaf whispered.

"Singing huh?" Angus said, waking up.

"I hear it," Erica said. She sounded scared.

The voice grew louder still.

Now they all heard what it was singing: *"Then the worms crawl in! And the worms crawl out! They'll eat your guts and then spit them out!"*

Angus gasped. "It's the executioner!"

Wiglaf slid out of his sleeping bag. He tiptoed over to the tent flap. He peeked outside. He didn't see a thing. But he heard the high voice more clearly now: *"They'll peel your skin!*

They'll drink your blood! Till all that's left are your bones in the mud!"

Erica began rattling the tools on her belt. "There must be something here I can use to make a ghost go away," she whispered.

Angus crawled over to Wiglaf. He, too, peeked out of the tent.

"There it is!" he whispered. He pointed with a shaky hand.

Wiglaf saw a shadowy shape.

"That can't be the executioner's ghost," Wiglaf told Angus. "It's too short."

"You'd be short, too, if you didn't have a head," Erica pointed out. "Call to it, Wiggie. Speak bravely. Maybe it won't harm us."

"Who...who...who goes there?" he said at last.

"Me!" called the shape.

"Me who?" Wiglaf called back.

"Me, Dudwin!"

Wiglaf gasped. He stuck his head out of the tent. "Dudwin?" he exclaimed. "Dudwin of Pinwick?"

"That's the one," the voice replied.

"Who is it, Wiglaf?" asked Erica. "What's going on?"

"Has he come to chop off our heads?" Angus whispered.

"It's not the ghost," Wiglaf said. "It's my little brother, Dudwin!"

Chapter 6

Wiglaf dashed out of the tent. He ran until he reached a sturdy boy of seven.

"Dudwin! It *is* you!" Wiglaf exclaimed. He saw that Dudwin had grown. And now—alas! His little brother was taller than he was!

Erica lit her mini-torch. She shone it on Wiglaf's brother. The boy had a round face and thick yellow hair. His tunic fit snugly over his belly. He wore baggy brown britches.

"Hallo, Wiggie!" Dudwin grinned. One front tooth was missing. He opened his arms and hugged Wiglaf—hard.

"Dudwin!" Wiglaf cried. "Let go!"

Dudwin did. "You smell like fish, Wiggie."

"What are you doing here, Dud?" Wiglaf asked, quickly changing the subject.

"I was on my way to your school," Dudwin explained. "Pa sent me. He wants me to bring him all the gold you've got so far."

"Oh, great!" Wiglaf said under his breath.

"Dudwin," said Erica. "Why were you singing that worm song?"

"I like that song," Dudwin said. "Another one I like is 'Greasy, Grimy Gopher Guts.' Oh, and speaking of greasy..." Dudwin took a large flask from his pack. "Ma sent you some of her cabbage soup."

"Egad!" Wiglaf exclaimed. "I hoped never to taste that soup again as long as I live!"

"I love cabbage soup!" Angus cried. "If you don't want it, I'll take it!" He grabbed the flask from Dudwin. He popped the cork. He took a sniff. "Eeeeeew!" he cried. "Wiglaf! Is your own mother trying to poison you?"

"Sometimes I wonder," Wiglaf said. "But it

was kind of her to send it." He took the flask, put the cork back in place, and handed it to his brother. "Hold onto it for me, Dud."

They walked back to camp. The sun was coming up, so there was no use trying to sleep now. Erica rubbed two dry sticks together and lit a fire. They all sat around it, warming their cold hands. Wiglaf wished that he did not have to give his brother bad news.

"Dudwin," he said at last, "you must go home empty-handed. I have no gold yet."

Dudwin frowned. "Father won't like that."

"No. But he will like this," Wiglaf said. "Tell him that *I* am a dragon slayer!"

"Oh, right!" Dudwin laughed loudly. He slapped Wiglaf on the back—hard. "Tell me another one, Wiggie!"

"Two dragons have died by my hand," Wiglaf said. "Well, more or less, by my hand."

"Aw, go on!" Dudwin shot back.

"It's true," Angus put in.

"For real?" Dudwin asked Erica.

Erica nodded. "I helped him, of course."

"But Wiggie hates the sight of blood," Dudwin said. "Back home, he wouldn't even swat a fly. Once he cut his thumb and fainted. He never—"

"Never mind!" Wiglaf cut in. "You must go home after breakfast, Dudwin. Tell Father that when I have gold, I shall bring it myself."

"But Father thinks I'll be gone for a week," Dudwin said. "I don't want to go home yet!"

"You must," Wiglaf said. "We are hunting dragon treasure. You would be in the way."

"No, I wouldn't!" Dudwin cried. "I can help you! I'm good at finding treasure. I found lots on my way here." He emptied his pockets. "Look!" he said. "I found a diamond!"

"That's a sparkly rock, Dudwin," Wiglaf said.

Dudwin ignored his brother. "Here is a spur from the boot of a knight!" he went on.

"That's nothing but a piece of a pinecone!" Wiglaf said.

"And here is the best treasure of all," the boy said happily. "The tip of a wizard's wand!"

"That, Dudwin," Wiglaf growled, "is a twig!"

"Lighten up, Wiglaf," Erica said with a laugh. "Dudwin has some fine treasures."

Dudwin grinned. "Yeah. Lighten up, Wiggie."

Wiglaf rolled his eyes.

"Let him stay, Wiglaf," Angus added. "Dudwin can be an honorary Bloodhound."

"Oh, boy!" Dudwin cried.

"We shall soon find Seetha's gold," Erica pointed out. "And Dudwin can take some straight home to your father."

"Yes, yes!" Dudwin cried.

"Four is better than three," Angus said. "Dudwin can help us carry our gear."

This last point won Wiglaf over. "All right, Dudwin," he told his brother. "You can stay."

Dudwin grinned. "I was going to anyway, Wiggie," he said.

After breakfast, Erica called, "Blood-hounds, march!"

"Wait!" Dudwin cried. "I see a goblin's hat!" He ran off and picked up an acorn cap.

Erica tapped her foot and waited for him to come back. Then off they went.

Wiglaf marched behind Dudwin. Deep down, he felt glad that his brother was with them. True, Dudwin could be a pain. But he had his good points. After all, he was carrying a heavy pack. And this meant Wiglaf's own pack was lighter.

That morning, the Bloodhounds hunted for Seetha's treasure in Bats-a-Plenty Cave. They searched Chock-Full-of-Spiders Cave. And Leeches-R-Us Cave. They looked for treasure in cave after cave. But they came out of each one empty-handed.

Except for Dudwin.

"Oh, boy!" he cried, sliding out of Slippery Cave. "I found a baby dragon's tooth!"

"That's a pebble, Dud," Wiglaf said.

"Here is a fine treasure!" Dudwin called inside Slimy Cave. "A goblet fit for a king!"

"Dudwin!" Erica cried. "You took that from my tool belt!" She grabbed her goblet back.

Erica marched the Bloodhounds from cave to cave. The day grew hot. The Bloodhounds began to sweat. Mosquitoes bit them.

As they started over the Shiver River Bridge, Angus called, "Let's stop for a swim!"

"Bloodhounds never stop!" Erica said.

But halfway across the bridge, Erica stopped. And Wiglaf saw why.

A great hairy arm, waving a big spiked club, was sticking up from under the bridge.

"Yikes!" Angus cried. "It's a troll!"

"Right!" the troll roared. He pulled himself up onto the bridge. "And this is my bridge!"

The troll's eyes darted from face to face. "Who wants me to eat them first?" he roared.

No Bloodhound volunteered. Not even Erica.

"Someone step forward!" cried the troll. "If I eat you all at once, I'll get a bellyache!"

No Bloodhound stepped forward.

"You are one ugly troll!" Dudwin shouted.

"Shush, Dudwin!" Wiglaf clapped a hand over his brother's mouth.

Erica drew her sword. "Back off, troll!"

"Make me!" the troll cried. He swung his club and knocked Erica's sword into the river.

"Alas!" Erica cried. "That was my special Sir Lancelot look-alike sword!"

The troll laughed. He reached out a long arm, snatched up Angus, and dangled him over his mouth.

"No! Don't eat me!" Angus cried. "I'll give you a *bad* bellyache!"

"Hey, Troll-breath!" Dudwin yelled.

"Dudwin, stop it!" Wiglaf cried.

Dudwin paid no attention. "I have something much yummier than him!" he shouted.

"What?" the troll growled.

"Cabbage soup," Dudwin answered.

The troll eyed Dudwin. "Homemade?" he asked.

Dudwin nodded. "By my own mother."

"Give it here," said the troll.

Dudwin pulled the flask from his pack.

"Don't, Dudwin!" Wiglaf begged. "Ma's soup will make him *really* mad!"

But Dudwin stepped bravely up to the troll. He popped the cork off the flask. A sickening smell filled the air. Dudwin quickly splashed the soup in the troll's face.

The troll's eyes grew wide with surprise. He stuck out his tongue and licked some of the soup from his face. "Mmmmmmm!" he growled.

Wiglaf gasped. "You like it?" he cried.

"Like it?" said the troll. "I love it!" He dropped Angus onto the bridge. "I'll eat you humans later. Now, I want more soup!"

"You got it!" Dudwin said. He threw the flask to the troll.

While the troll gulped down the soup, the Bloodhounds ran across his bridge. They kept running until the troll was far behind. Then they fell down, gasping for breath.

"Nice work, Dudwin!" Erica exclaimed.

"*Very* nice," Angus said. "How is it that you were brave enough to stand up to the troll?"

"Oh, all my brothers are much meaner than the troll," Dudwin said. "Except for Wiglaf."

Wiglaf patted his brother on the back. He was proud of Dudwin. But at the same time, he felt—well, ashamed. His little brother was taller than he was. His little brother carried a bigger pack. And now his little brother had saved them from the troll. It was hard to take.

While Angus rested after his near-death-by-troll experience, Dudwin ran off. He was gone for a long time. Wiglaf was starting to worry when he came running back.

"Eric!" Dudwin cried. "Look what I found!"

"Shhh," Erica said. "I'm checking the map."

Dudwin ran over to Angus. "Look at this!" he exclaimed.

"Don't bother me, Dudwin," Angus said. "Not after what I've been through."

Dudwin turned to his brother. "Wiggie?"

Wiglaf sighed. "What did you find, Dud?"

Dudwin held out his hand to Wiglaf.

"Egad!" cried Wiglaf.

For there in Dudwin's grubby hand lay two golden coins.

Chapter 7

"**G**old coins!" Wiglaf cried. "Where did you find them, Dudwin?"

"Gold?" Erica exclaimed. "Did you say *gold*?" She and Angus hurried over.

"I found them—" Dudwin began eagerly. Then he stopped. A strange look came over his face. "I'm not telling," he said.

"What?" Erica cried. "Why not?"

"Because," Dudwin said, "you keep making fun of my treasure."

"Don't be that way, Dudwin," Erica said. "Seetha must have dropped the coins on her way to her secret hiding place. Show us where you found them. The Cave of Doom will be close by. Come on, Dudwin!"

But Dudwin only shook his head *no*.

Erica pulled Wiglaf and Angus aside. "He's *your* brother, Wiglaf," Erica said in a low voice so Dudwin couldn't hear. "Make him tell!"

Wiglaf rolled his eyes. "What do you want me to do? Torture him?"

"If that's what it takes," Erica shot back.

Wiglaf really wanted to find the gold. If he did, he wouldn't have to send Dudwin home empty-handed. And he was sure Mordred would stop picking on him. He had to get Dudwin to tell where he found the coins so they could find the cave. He thought hard.

"Dudwin is stubborn," he told Erica at last. "Talking to him will do no good. But try offering him something from your tool belt."

Erica gasped. "I saved up for six months to buy this tool belt! Why should I be the one to bribe Dudwin?"

"Because you are the only one with anything to trade," Angus pointed out.

They walked back over to Dudwin.

"Dudwin," Erica said, "show us where you found the coins. If you do, I shall give you a tool from my Sir Lancelot Tool Belt."

"Oh, boy!" Dudwin cried. "Which one?"

"Well..." Erica said. "The toothpick."

Dudwin shook his head.

"The lice comb?"

"No way," Dudwin said.

Erica sighed. "What do you want?"

Dudwin grinned. "The torch."

"What?" Erica cried. "That is my best tool!"

Dudwin jingled the coins in his pocket.

Erica took the torch from her belt. She looked at it longingly. Then she handed it to Dudwin.

"Oh, boy!" Dudwin exclaimed. "Now I can find treasures in the dark!"

"Cut the chitchat," Erica snapped. "Show us where you found the coins."

Dudwin led the way through the forest. He stopped at the foot of a big hill, covered with vines. "There," he said.

"Clear the brush, Bloodhounds!" Erica ordered. "Keep a look out for coins!"

Wiglaf and Angus drew their swords. They began hacking away at the vines. But they found that the vines were not really growing on the hill. They had only been piled up there as if to hide something. The boys pulled the vines away and discovered a great hole in the side of the hill.

"It's the mouth of a cave!" cried Angus.

Wiglaf's eyes grew wide. Pointed rocks hung down over the cave entrance. It looked exactly like the open mouth of a dragon!

A wooden sign had fallen face down beside the entrance. Wiglaf picked it up. It said:

WELCOME TO
THE CAVE OF DOOM!

Wiglaf quickly dropped the sign. They had found the Cave of Doom!

"Footprints!" Erica cried suddenly. "Going into the cave!" She studied the prints with her magnifying glass. "They're Seetha's, all right," she said. "I'm going in. Who's going with me?"

"Not me," said Angus.

"Me!" cried Dudwin.

"No, Dud," Wiglaf said. "You stay out here with Angus. I—I'll go in."

"But it's dark in the cave." Dudwin held up the torch. "And I have the light."

"Good point," Erica said. "And very brave of you to want to come." She shot Angus a look.

"Oh, all right," Angus said. "I'll come, too."

"All right, Bloodhounds," Erica said. "Let's go in!"

"Not so fast!" called a voice behind them. "Not so fast!"

Wiglaf whirled around. There, sitting on his thronelike chair, was Mordred!

"Greetings, Bloodhounds!" Mordred smiled at them. None of the skinny student teachers were smiling. They were struggling to put their heavy headmaster down gently.

"I have come to see how you are doing," Mordred said. "Where is Plungett?"

"He had an accident, Uncle," Angus said. "The Marley brothers took him back to DSA."

"Egad!" Mordred cried. "I hope he is not hurt badly. It would not be easy to find a new slaying coach. Not at the salary I pay." His violet eyes lit upon Dudwin. "And who, pray tell, is *this?*"

"Dudwin," Wiglaf answered. "My brother."

"Why in the name of King Ken's britches is your big brother here?" Mordred barked.

"He's my *little* brother," Wiglaf said. "But, sir! We have found Seetha's hiding spot. Somewhere inside this cave is her gold."

Wiglaf had said the magic word: gold.

Mordred jumped down from his chair. "Oh, joy!" he cried. "Oh, happy day! Come! I shall lead you into the cave myself!"

Mordred took a step toward the dark mouth of the cave. Then he stopped.

"On second thought," he said, "I shall *follow* you Bloodhounds into the cave. That way I can make sure nothing sneaks up on you from behind." Mordred pointed at Dudwin. "You with the torch!" he said. "Lead the way!"

"To the treasure!" Dudwin yelled. And he ran into the cave.

Wiglaf, Erica, and Angus hurried after him. The torchlight threw tall shadows onto the stony walls. High above Wiglaf's head long, thin stalactites hung down from the ceiling. There were hundreds of them. They looked like stone fangs!

"Don't dawdle!" Mordred called from behind. "Do you see any sign of the gold?"

"Not yet, sir!" Erica called back.

Suddenly Dudwin tripped. The torch flew from his hand as he fell.

Wiglaf reached down to help him up. As he picked up the torch, he saw that his brother had fallen over a pile of white shapes. It took him a moment to understand what they were.

"B-b-b-bones!" Wiglaf cried.

"Bones?" Angus screamed. He took off for the mouth of the cave.

"Oof!" Mordred grunted as his nephew ran into him. He grabbed Angus's arm.

"Let go!" Angus cried. "I'm out of here!"

"Are you mad?" Mordred roared. "We're so close to Seetha's gold, I can almost smell it!"

"I think that smell is dried bat droppings, sir," Erica offered.

"Whatever," Mordred said. He turned Angus around. "Onward!"

"Whose bones are they, Wiggie?" Dudwin asked as they began inching forward.

"Some big animal probably died here long ago," Wiglaf said. He hoped it was true.

"I want to keep some," Dudwin said. He began picking up bones.

"What's the holdup?" Mordred yelled from the back of the line. "Go! Go! Go!"

"What's this?" Erica said. She bent down. But instead of a bone, she picked up a hat.

Wiglaf stared at the thing in Erica's hand. "What is stuck in that hat?" he asked.

"Looks like a red-and-white striped turkey feather," Erica answered. "And it is the prettiest darn feather I ever did see."

"This must be Crazy Looey's hat!" Wiglaf

cried. "And these bones! They must be the bones of his seven brave men!"

"Move!" Mordred called. "Moooove!"

"We are doomed!" Angus howled.

"I'm too young to get doomed!" Dudwin cried. The torchlight wavered as his hand began to shake. "I want to go back, Wiggie!"

"Be brave, Dudwin," Wiglaf whispered. "You are a Bloodhound now. And Bloodhounds never turn back. Besides," he added, "Mordred won't let you turn back."

Wiglaf untied his lucky rag from his sword.

"Here, Dudwin," he said, handing it to him. "This has always brought me luck. I am sure it will keep you from being doomed."

"Thanks, Wiggie." Dudwin sniffed. He held the rag tightly as he began walking again.

Erica started singing in a shaky voice: *"We're the mighty Bloodhounds...We're dogged and we're bold..."*

The others joined in. Their voices echoed as they walked toward a faint yellow glow far back in the cave. They followed Dudwin through a passageway. They came out in a big open space lit by a strange, yellow light.

Wiglaf blinked. And then he saw before him a life-sized statue of Seetha! Her wings were spread. Her tail was curled around a giant stone bowl. And piled high in the bowl were bright, shining golden coins!

Mordred pushed past Wiglaf. "Gold!" he cried. Tears of joy sprang to his eyes. "A mountain of gold! And it all belongs to ME!"

Chapter 8

"Don't start counting your gold yet, sir!" Wiglaf said. "Look! Seetha has left us a message on the wall!" And he began to read what had been scratched in stone:

If I die, I, Seetha von Flambé, leave all my gold to my 3,683 children. To anyone else who finds my gold—anyone who is NOT one of my beautiful children—I leave this warning:

GO AWAY! GO FAR AWAY!
DO NOT COME BACK SOME OTHER DAY!
FOR IF YOU STEAL A COIN — JUST ONE...
YOU'LL MEET YOUR DOOM —

IT WON'T BE FUN.
SMOKE WILL CHOKE YOU!
FIRES WILL BLAZE!
THE CAVE WILL SHAKE!
YOU'LL BE AMAZED!
SPEARS SHALL RAIN DOWN FROM ON HIGH!
AND <u>YOU</u> SHALL BE THE NEXT TO DIE!

"I'm scared!" Dudwin cried.

"Me, too!" Angus said.

Wiglaf started shaking.

Even Erica looked scared.

"Don't be such sausages!" Mordred cried. "What else would a dragon say? 'Go ahead. Help yourself to all my gold!' I don't think so!"

"Please Uncle Mordred!" Angus fell to his knees. "Let's get out of here! I beg you! Seetha may be dead. But she means business!"

"Fiddlesticks!" Mordred barked. "Stop stalling, all of you! Go get my gold!"

Then, to Wiglaf's horror, Dudwin spoke up. "You're the one who wants the gold," he told Mordred. "So why don't you get it yourself?"

"What?" roared Mordred. "Me? Don't you know why boys were invented? So grown-ups never have to do anything they don't want to! Now, *go get my gold!*"

The Bloodhounds stayed close together. They inched toward the bowl of treasure.

"Okay," said Erica when they reached it. "Who shall take the first coin from the pile?"

Wiglaf swallowed. Here was a chance for him to do a brave deed. Besides, if taking a coin set off a booby trap, what did it matter who took it? They were all goners.

"I'll do it," Wiglaf said. He drew a breath. Slowly he slid a coin from the pile. He waited for the smoke and fire.

But nothing happened.

Mordred cried, "What did I tell you, boys? Seetha's warning was pure poppycock!"

Then Wiglaf heard a low rumble.

"Is that your stomach?" he asked Erica.

"No," she said. "I thought it was yours."

The rumbling grew louder.

"Ohhh!" howled Angus. "It's doom time!"

Wiglaf swallowed. He quickly tossed the coin back onto the pile of gold.

Too late!

The rumbling thundered louder. Then the gold in the big stone bowl started to spin around and around. It quickly picked up speed. The coins circled the bowl faster and faster. Then, as if someone had pulled a plug at the bottom of the bowl, the coins began to disappear down a hole. *SLUUUUUURP!*

"What's happening?" Mordred cried.

"The gold is going down some kind of drain!" Angus answered.

"WHAT?" Mordred screamed. And he started running toward the stone dragon.

The Bloodhounds jumped out of the way as the headmaster took a flying leap into the bowl. He slid down, grabbing for the coins.

There was a final *SLURP!* Then it was still.

"All is not lost!" Mordred cried happily. "I have a great big handful of gold!"

Mordred tried to pull his arm out. But his fist, full of coins, was stuck in the hole.

"Help me, lads!" Mordred cried.

The Bloodhounds held onto Mordred's boots. They pulled with all their might. At last...*POP!* Off came the boots.

"You ninnies!" Mordred cried. "Pull *me!*"

The Bloodhounds grabbed Mordred's feet. They pulled as hard as they could. But his fist stayed stuck.

"Stop," Mordred cried at last. "Leave me here, boys. Carry on at DSA as best you can without me. It won't be easy. But you must try!"

"But Uncle Mor—" Angus began.

"No, nephew," Mordred said. "Do not try to comfort me. My death will be slow. Slow and very terrible. But I shall be brave and—"

"Sir?" Erica cut in.

"Quiet!" Mordred snapped. "As I was saying, I shall be brave. And so it is fitting that one of the DSA towers be named for me. The north one, I think. Mordred's Tower. That has a nice ring to it."

"You don't have to die here, sir!" Wiglaf said. "You *can* save yourself!"

"Blazing King Ken's britches!" Mordred cried. "Are you going to pester me to death? Well, tell me, boy. How can I save myself?"

And Wiglaf said, "Let go of the gold."

"Let go?" Mordred looked puzzled.

"Yes, Uncle!" Angus answered. "Then your hand can slide out of the hole."

Mordred frowned. "You cannot mean I should give up the gold? No. Never."

Wiglaf turned to Erica. "We have to get out of here!" he said. "What shall we do?"

"I don't know," Erica said. "But Sir Lancelot will." She yanked *The Sir Lancelot Handbook* from her belt. She began turning pages. "Ah ha!" she cried happily. "Here, under 'Emergencies.'" She began to read aloud: *"Emergency #54: Is there a great big greedy man whose hand is stuck down a hole because he won't let go of a fist full of gold coins?"*

"Yes!" cried Angus. "Yes! That's it exactly!"

"If the great big greedy man doesn't hurry up and let go," Erica read on, *"are you in danger of being doomed?"*

"Yes!" Angus cried. "Right again!"

Erica read on. *"When all else fails..."*

She turned the page. *"...try tickling!"*

"Oh, boy!" Dudwin cried.

Then all four Bloodhounds jumped on Mordred.

"Stop!" cried Mordred. "What are you doing?"

"Sorry, sir," Erica said. She was tickling his belly. "But it's for your own good."

"Hoo-hoo!" Mordred howled. "Oh! Stop!"

No one stopped. Angus tickled Mordred's left foot. Wiglaf did the same to his right. Dudwin chucked him under the chin.

Mordred wiggled and giggled. He kicked and screamed, "Have mercy!"

But the Bloodhounds kept on. At last Wiglaf heard *Clink! Clink! Clink!* as the coins fell from Mordred's fist.

"It worked!" he cried.

"Of course it did!" Erica exclaimed. "Sir Lancelot has never let me down!"

"Noooo!" Mordred sobbed as his hand—his empty hand—popped out of the hole. He pushed away the ticklers. His eyes glowed with red-hot fury.

"Trick *me* out of my gold, will you?" he cried. He pulled on his boots. "Wait till I get my hands on you!"

"But, sir!" Erica said. "We couldn't leave you here to die!"

"Don't argue with him!" Wiglaf said. "Let's go!"

"Wait!" Dudwin yelled. "I spy treasure!"

"Treasure?" Mordred cried. "Where?"

Dudwin pushed the torch into Wiglaf's hand. Then he started climbing up the dragon statue.

"Stop!" Wiglaf cried. "Dudwin! Come back down!"

But Dudwin kept climbing. And now Wiglaf saw why. Between its stone teeth, the dragon statue held one last gold coin.

Mordred's eyes lit up as he saw it, too. He lunged for the statue.

"There is just one coin, boy!" the headmaster roared. "Just one! And it's mine!"

One coin. Just one. Seetha's warning rang inside Wiglaf's head.

FOR IF YOU STEAL A COIN—JUST ONE...
YOU'LL MEET YOUR DOOM—
IT WON'T BE FUN.

Now Wiglaf understood. Seetha's warning was about one coin—just one! And suddenly he knew that the warning wasn't poppycock at all.

"Don't touch that coin!" Wiglaf yelled to the climbers. "Don't touch it!"

Too late! Mordred had already snatched the coin from between the dragon's teeth.

"Ha ha!" he cried. "I got it first! I got—"

Mordred got no further.

A flame shot from the statue's mouth.

"Yowie!" Mordred cried. He jumped down.

Dudwin jumped down, too.

Smoke began to pour from the stone dragon's nose. More flames shot from between its jaws. The cave walls began to shake.

THWUNK! A stalactite dropped from the ceiling.

Wiglaf stared at the quivering stone spear in front of him. It had missed him by inches!

THWUNK! Another dropped beside him.

THWUNK! And another!

And then, just as Seetha had warned, hundreds of stone spears began raining down.

"Help!" cried Angus. "We're doomed!"

Chapter 9

Wiglaf grabbed Dudwin's hand. He ran through the smoke, pulling his brother with him.

THWUNK! A stalactite landed right behind them.

Wiglaf dropped the torch. It hit the cave floor and sputtered out. The cave was dark now. And filled with smoke. Wiglaf could hardly breathe. But he kept going. Far off, he thought he saw light. The mouth of the cave!

THWUNK!

Wiglaf jumped back from the stalactite. Dudwin's hand slid out of his.

THWUNK! THWUNK! THWUNK!

Stone spears were falling thick and fast! Wiglaf ran for his life. He thought his brother was ahead of him. "Run toward the light, Dudwin!" he yelled.

Wiglaf heard a *whoosh* as Mordred raced by him.

At last, Wiglaf reached the mouth of the cave. He ran out into the daylight, gasping for air.

He saw Erica. And Mordred was leaning against the student teachers, catching his breath. But where was Dudwin?

Wiglaf heard footsteps. That had to be his brother. But a second later, Angus ran out of the cave.

"I'm not doomed after all!" Angus cried.

Wiglaf ran back to the mouth of the cave. "Dudwin?" he called. "Are you in there?"

"I'm stuck!" came the faint reply. "Help me, Wiggie!"

"I'm coming!" Wiglaf raced back into the cave. Falling stalactites whistled by him.

"Over here, Wiggie!" the boy cried.

Wiglaf turned toward the voice. At last he found his brother. A stalactite had stabbed through Dudwin's baggy britches, pinning him to the spot.

Wiglaf tugged on the stalactite. He pulled with all his might. But it stayed stuck.

"Step out of your breeches, Dud," Wiglaf said. "Hurry! You'll have to leave them here."

"No way!" Dudwin cried. "My treasures are in my pockets."

Wiglaf groaned. He didn't have time to argue. He felt like giving his stubborn little brother a kick in the shin. Instead, he drew back his foot and kicked the stalactite—hard!

Snap! It broke off at the base.

"Ooooh!" Wiglaf cried. Had he broken all his toes, too?

"Way to go, Wiggie!" cried Dudwin.

Wiglaf grabbed Dudwin again. He forgot about his throbbing toes as he pulled his brother toward the light.

Then, to his horror, he saw that stone spears were falling right inside the mouth of the cave. And falling fast! The entrance was almost blocked!

"Faster, Dud!" Wiglaf cried. "Faster!" Wiglaf pushed Dudwin—hard! His brother half flew out of the cave.

Wiglaf dove after him. He rolled away as the spears filled the mouth of the cave. He lay on the ground, panting.

Dudwin raced over to Wiglaf. He helped him up. He threw his arms around him.

"Wiglaf!" he cried. "You saved my life!"

"Pipe down, you blasted boys!" Mordred yelled. "If not for you, I'd be a rich man!"

"A rich *dead* man," Angus added.

Dudwin ran over to Mordred. "I want to be

like my brave big brother! I want to go to Dragon Slayers' Academy. Can I? Please?"

"You must be joking!" Mordred cried. "Wiglaf still owes me his seven pennies. You think I would let his brother in for free?"

"I can pay!" Dudwin said. He reached into his pocket. He pulled out his two gold coins.

Mordred's eyes almost popped out of his head. "Those are *my* coins!" he roared. "I dropped them! Right in the spot where you found them!"

Dudwin said pulled his hand back. "I'm not falling for *that* old trick!"

"Give him one coin, Dud," Wiglaf whispered. "Or you shall lose both of them."

"If you say so, Wiglaf," Dudwin said.

And he threw one coin in a bush.

Mordred dove after it.

"Now run home with the other coin," Wiglaf said. "Quickly, Dud! Before Mordred tries to get his hands on it!"

Dudwin slipped the coin into his pocket. He picked up his pack. He gave Wiglaf back his lucky rag. "It worked, Wiggie," Dudwin said. "I didn't get doomed."

"Farewell, Dudwin!" Wiglaf said.

"Good-bye, Wiggie!" Dudwin smiled. "I'll tell them at home how you saved my life in the Cave of Doom! I'll tell them you are a hero!"

Dudwin waved and took off for the road.

Mordred crawled out from under the bush. He held up the gold coin. "Got it!" he cried.

"Excuse me, sir?" Erica said.

"What now?" Mordred asked as he got to his feet.

"We Bloodhounds found Seetha's gold," Erica said. "So we should get the prize."

"Oh! You want a prize, do you?" Mordred showed all his teeth in a fierce grin. "And so you shall have one!"

Wiglaf didn't like the way Mordred said that.

"Student teachers!" Mordred called. "Take the rest of the day off."

"Oh, thank you, sir!" cried the thin ones.

Mordred stomped over to his throne-like chair. He sat down.

"Wiglaf, for your prize, take the right front pole!" he ordered. "Eric, left front! Angus, you take the two in the rear! Pick me up all at once, boys. No bouncing!"

Wiglaf struggled to pick up his part of the large headmaster. He groaned as he took a step.

"Faster, boys!" Mordred cried. "Or we shall never make it home by nightfall!"

"Things could be worse," Erica said bravely as they staggered toward DSA.

Wiglaf nodded. And once they got there, he thought, they probably would be. But for now

Wiglaf felt glad that he had sent his brother home with a gold coin. And with a true story about Wiglaf, the hero.

This time he started the singing:

> *"We're the mighty Bloodhounds!*
> *We're dogged and we're bold!*
> *We're the mighty Bloodhounds!*
> *And we found Seetha's gold!"*

A WEDDING
FOR WIGLAF?

For Audrey Kubetin
—K.H. McM.

Dragon Slayers' Academy ™ 4

A WEDDING
FOR WIGLAF?

By K.H. McMullan
Illustrated by Bill Basso

GROSSET & DUNLAP • NEW YORK

Library of Congress Cataloging-in-Publication Data

McMullan, K.H.

A wedding for Wiglaf / by K.H. McMullan ; illustrated by Bill Basso.

p. cm. — (Dragon Slayers' Academy ; 4)

Summary: When the headmaster of the Dragon Slayers' Academy hears that Princess Belcheena will pay the matchmaker who finds her a husband, he decides that Wiglaf is the perfect candidate.

[1. Princesses—Fiction. 2. Weddings—Fiction. 3. Schools—Fiction.] I. Basso, Bill, ill.
II. Series: McMullan, K.H. Dragon Slayers Academy ; 4.
PZ7.M47879We 1998
[Fic]—dc21
                                                                                    98-41532
                                                                                    CIP
ISBN 0-448-42290-5   A B C D E F G H I J   AC

Chapter I

Wiglaf pushed his carrot-colored hair off his sweaty brow. It was a hot spring day. Coach Plungett had given his class a break to get a drink. Wiglaf and the other students stood in line at the well in the castle yard, waiting for a turn with the dipper.

Coach leaned against the well. "I've killed many a dragon, lads," he said. "Ah, yes...but I'll never forget the first. You never do. Hotblaze was his name. The beast spewed flames so hot they melted my helmet. Burned my hair off, too. Been bald as a potato ever since. But that didn't stop me. I drew my sword like a manly man! I jabbed Hotblaze in his left flank. Or...was it his right?" Coach pushed back his brown, pageboy-style wig. He scratched his hairless head, trying to think.

Wiglaf hoped Coach wouldn't go on and on, telling how Hotblaze met his end. Blood-and-guts stories always made him feel sick to his stomach.

"Wiglaf!" someone called.

Wiglaf turned. He saw his friend Angus hurrying across the castle yard.

"Uncle Mordred wants to see you in his office right away!" Angus yelled.

Me? Wiglaf pointed to himself.

"Go on, lad," Coach told Wiglaf. "You can get the homework from Torblad."

"Nice knowing you, Wiglaf," Torblad scoffed.

Wiglaf trotted off. He was glad to get out of class. But he hated to think why he was being summoned by the hot-tempered headmaster of Dragon Slayers' Academy.

Mordred was not fond of Wiglaf. For Wiglaf had, quite by accident, killed two dragons, Gorzil and Seetha. But he had not brought Mordred any of their dragon gold.

Wiglaf caught up with Angus. "What does Mordred want?" he asked. The two began hurrying toward the old castle that housed DSA.

Angus shrugged. "Uncle Mordred didn't say. But he wasn't angry. In fact, he seemed rather...jolly."

"Jolly?" Wiglaf exclaimed. That was a new one. Mordred was never jolly.

The boys ran all the way to Mordred's office. Angus knocked on the door.

"Enter!" boomed a voice.

The boys entered. They found Mordred standing next to his desk, reading a copy of

The Medieval Times. He wore a red velvet tunic with golden dragons stitched on it.

"Ah, Wiglaf!" Mordred put down his newspaper. "Back to work, Angus," he added, never taking his violet eyes from Wiglaf. "I don't pay you half a penny a year to stand around gawking!"

"No, Uncle," Angus said. He went back to polishing the headmaster's big black boots.

"Ah, Wiglaf!" Mordred exclaimed again. "How are you feeling, my boy? Fit as a fiddle, I hope?"

"Yes, thank you, sir," Wiglaf answered. He wondered why the headmaster had asked. Mordred was not one to worry about the health of his students. Quite the opposite, in fact.

"And your pet pig," Mordred went on. "Is Daisy happy living out in the henhouse?"

"Very happy, sir," Wiglaf answered.

It surprised him that Mordred knew about

Daisy. He had brought his dear pig to school with him from his home in Pinwick. He wondered if Mordred also knew that Daisy was under a wizard's spell. She could speak—in Pig Latin.

"Is Frypot feeding you enough lumpen pudding?" Mordred asked.

"More than enough, sir," Wiglaf said.

"Excuse me, Uncle Mordred," Angus said. He held up a boot. "Is this shiny enough for you?"

"You must be joking!" Mordred yelled. "Put some elbow grease into it, nephew!"

Angus sighed and went back to polishing.

"Now, about clothes, Wiglaf," Mordred said. "My sister Lobelia will order you a new tunic. And fine new britches, too."

"Clothes?" Wiglaf said. "But I have no money! I cannot pay for new clothes."

"Worry not, my boy," Mordred said, still smiling. "I shall pay for everything!"

Wiglaf gasped. Now he understood. Mordred had lost his mind!

The DSA headmaster was a famous penny pincher. He never spent a cent if he could help it. He would never, in a million years, pay for anything for anybody else. Especially not for Wiglaf.

There was a sudden knock on the door.

"Enter!" Mordred said.

The door flew open. Erica ran into the office. Erica dressed as a boy so she could go to DSA. Everyone there called her Eric. Wiglaf was the only student who knew that she was a girl. And a royal one at that. She was none other than Princess Erica, daughter of Queen Barb and King Ken.

"Sir!" Erica cried. "Come quickly! Torblad fell into the moat. And he cannot swim!"

"Torblad, eh?" Mordred scratched his chin thoughtfully. "I wonder if he is all paid up.

Let me check my records." He opened a worn leather book. On the cover, it said:

MORDRED'S MONEY

Private! Keep Out! No Peeking! I Mean It!

"Hmmm. Just as I thought," the headmaster muttered. "Torblad owes me for two semesters." Mordred jumped up suddenly. "Egad!" he cried. "If he drowns, I'll never see a penny of it! Wait here, Wiglaf. I'll be back!" The headmaster raced from the room. Erica raced after him.

Wiglaf turned to Angus. "Your uncle has gone mad!" he said. "Why else would he offer to buy me new clothes?"

"Oh, he has something up his sleeve," Angus said. "You can be sure of that." He put down the boot he was polishing. He picked up Mordred's copy of *The Medieval Times*. "Let's see if Dragon Stabbers' Prep beat Knights-R-Us in the jousting match," he said.

"Wait," said Wiglaf. "What's this on the front page?" Together, the boys read the headline story.

BELCHEENA WORTH BILLIONS
Super-Rich Princess Seeks Husband
EAST ARMPITTSIA Wednesday, June 8—

Years ago, Princess Belcheena's heart was broken. The love of her life rode off, never to be seen again. The princess shut herself up in her tower in Mildew Palace. She comforted herself by counting her gold. She has great mountains of it, so counting it took a long time. But last week, she finished. Now the princess has come out into the world again. And she is looking for a husband.

"I have over twelve billion in gold coins," the princess told reporters on Monday. "Now all I need is a special someone to help me spend it. Princes seek wives all the time," she added. "Why shouldn't a princess seek a husband?"

There are three things the princess is looking for in her future groom. He must be a dragon slayer.

He must be a redhead. And his name must begin with Princess Belcheena's favorite letter of the alphabet—W.

"The matchmaker who finds me the right husband will get a pot of gold," the princess promised.

Angus whistled. "Belcheena is loaded!"

"I wonder why her true love rode away," Wiglaf said.

Just then the door swung open. Mordred was back. His hair and his tunic dripped with foul-smelling moat water.

"Torblad is saved," he growled. "But he had better pay up soon. Or I'll throw the little rotter back into the moat myself."

Mordred glanced at Angus and Wiglaf. "Ah, you've seen the paper!" he said. "I guess my little surprise is out of the bag. Eh, Wiglaf?"

"Your surprise, sir?" Wiglaf asked.

"Yes, my boy," Mordred said happily. "You are about to get married!"

Chapter 2

"Excuse me, sir?" Wiglaf managed. "I don't think I heard you right."

"You...are...about...to...get...married," Mordred said again.

Wiglaf looked over his shoulder. Mordred had to be speaking to someone behind him.

But there was no one behind him.

"You cannot mean Wiglaf," Angus said.

"Oh, but I do!" Mordred picked up the paper. "Belcheena says her husband must be a dragon slayer. And Wiglaf has slain two dragons."

"But only by accident, sir!" Wiglaf cried. "Surely the princess wants a husband who slew his dragons on purpose."

"Fiddle-faddle," Mordred said. He glanced at the paper again. "Belcheena wants a red-headed husband. And you, Wiglaf, are a red-head."

"My hair is orange, sir," Wiglaf pointed out.

"Close enough," Mordred growled. "Next you will tell me that Wiglaf does not begin with *W!*"

"No, sir," Wiglaf said miserably.

"Well then!" Mordred boomed. "It looks as if I shall be a matchmaker! And I shall get the pot of gold!" He rubbed his hands together. "Ha! I knew there was an easier way to get rich than sending half-witted boys out to bring me dragon gold!"

Mordred glanced at the sundial on his desk. "Off with you now, Wiglaf," he said. "Come back after supper tonight. Lobelia will be here then. And we'll make plans for your wedding!"

Wiglaf fell to his knees. "I am a peasant!" he

cried. "My twelve brothers smell bad, for my father thinks bathing causes madness! My—"

"Say no more, Wiglaf," Mordred cut him off. "I understand what you are telling me."

"Oh, do you, sir?" Wiglaf cried happily.

"Certainly," Mordred said. "You don't want to invite your family to the wedding."

"Uh...that is not exactly what I meant, sir," Wiglaf said. "I was trying to explain how very unfit I am to mar...mar..." He could not bring himself to say the awful word! "How unfit I am for a princess," he said at last.

Mordred frowned. "You are a redheaded dragon slayer named Wiglaf. You are exactly what the princess wants. I shall make this known to her. And I shall get the pot of gold. I wonder," he added dreamily, "just how big a pot it is?"

Mordred stared into space, imagining his pot of gold. The boys quietly left his office. They headed for Scrubbing Class.

"Can your uncle really make me get mar... mar..." Try as he might, Wiglaf could not say it! "Can he make me do this thing?" Wiglaf asked.

"He seems to think so," Angus said.

They walked in silence for a while. Then Angus said, "Do not take this the wrong way, Wiglaf. But when the princess sees you, surely she will put a stop to any wedding."

"I hope you're right," Wiglaf said. But he was worried. Mordred was so set on getting that pot of gold.

The boys reached the DSA kitchen. Frypot stood at the door. "Hurry in to class, boys," he called. "You may think Scrubbing is not as exciting as Slaying Class. But wait until you make a kill. It's a mess, what with the dragon guts hanging off your sword and all. Then you'll be glad you took old Frypot's Scrubbing Class."

Wiglaf hurried over to Erica on the far side

of the room. She was scraping burned lumpen pudding from a big pot. *How like Erica to pick the dirtiest pot,* Wiglaf thought. No wonder she always won the Dragon Slayer of the Month medal.

"Wiglaf!" Erica cried when she saw him. "What were you doing in Mordred's office?"

"I'll tell you," Wiglaf whispered. "But first I must ask you something. Do you princesses—"

"Talk not of princesses!" Erica hissed. "If you have breathed a word of my secret, Wiglaf..."

"I have said nothing!" Wiglaf said. "I swear it on my sword!"

"Ha!" Erica scoffed. "That rusty old thing?"

"I shall never tell your secret," Wiglaf said. "But tell me! Do you know Belcheena?"

"Belcheena!" Erica cried.

Several heads turned toward them.

"Shhhh!" Wiglaf whispered. "What is she like?"

"Belcheena doesn't come out of her tower much," Erica said. "But I saw her once at a Princess Talent Contest. That was the day I won first prize in sword fighting! True, only one other princess had entered, but I—"

"What about Belcheena?" Wiglaf put in.

"As I remember, she sang a sad song. 'The Squire of My Desire,' I think. Why do you ask, Wiglaf?"

"There is a story about her in the paper," Wiglaf said. "She is looking for a husband."

"Belcheena is very..." Erica stopped for a moment. "How shall I put it? Belcheena has a very strong personality. I pity the man who marries her."

"Then you may have to pity me!" Wiglaf cried. And he told Erica all that had taken place in Mordred's office.

"I have no wish to marry *anyone*," Wiglaf finished up. "I want to stay here at DSA with my friends. I want to become a knight some-day. I want to travel the kingdom, helping villagers. And saving small, helpless animals—"

"Yes, yes," Erica broke in. "So tell Mordred that you won't marry Belcheena."

"But she has promised a pot of gold to the matchmaker who finds her a redheaded, dragon-slaying, *W*-named husband," Wiglaf said. "And Mordred has his heart set on this pot."

"Ah," Erica said. "Mordred is after her gold, is he? Well then, if I were you, Wiggie, I know what I'd be doing right now."

"What?" Wiglaf cried. "Tell me!"

Erica smiled. "I'd be picking out the perfect spot for my honeymoon!"

Chapter 3

The lumpen pudding that night was even worse than usual. Frypot had burned it to a crisp. But he hacked the blackened glop to pieces and served it anyway.

After supper, Wiglaf felt sick. But he didn't know if it was from the pudding or the thought of getting mar...mar... Oh, he could not even think it! Slowly he made his way to Mordred's office.

Mordred beamed as he let Wiglaf in. "Here he is, Lobelia. The lucky groom!"

Lobelia smiled. She had violet eyes and thick dark hair like Mordred. But there the likeness between brother and sister ended.

Lobelia was thin and known for her high style.

"Sit, Wiglaf," Mordred said.

Wiglaf sat down across from Mordred's desk.

"I have written to Belcheena." Mordred handed Wiglaf a sheet of parchment. "This is a first draft. Read it—quickly! I shall have Brother Dave up in the—oh, what do you call that room in the tower with all the books?"

"The library," Wiglaf said.

"Yes, yes," Mordred said. "Brother Dave up in the library will copy it over. Then I shall send it off to Belcheena."

Wiglaf's hand shook as he held the letter:

Wednesday, June 8

To Her Royal Ri~~ckness~~ Highness,

Princess Bil~~kons~~ Belcheena, Mildew Palace, East Armpittsia

Dear Princess ~~Bil~~ Belcheena:

I have read of your search for a husband. I know

such a ~~boy~~ ~~man~~ ~~twerp~~ person as you describe. He has killed two dragons. His hair is red. His name is Wiglaf of Pinwick.

As you can see, he meets all your requirements. So come and marry him. Do not delay. His heart ~~thumps~~ ~~clonks~~ ~~pounds~~ ~~beats~~ pitter-patters with love for you already.

Your number one matchmaker,

Mordred the Marvelous, Headmaster DSA

P.S. Wiglaf is perfect for you. So go ahead and bring along that great big pot of gold.

Wiglaf's heart indeed thumped, clonked, pounded, beat, and pitter-pattered. Not with love. But with fear that this awful thing might really happen!

Lobelia skimmed the letter. "Very nice, Mordie," she said when she finished.

Mordred smiled. He pulled a velvet bell cord hanging on the wall. A DSA student teacher quickly appeared at the door.

"Take this to Brother Dave." Mordred handed him the letter. "Wait while he copies it. Then give the copy to my scout, Yorick. Tell him to deliver it to Mildew Palace tonight."

Tonight! Wiglaf gulped. Things were moving quickly. Way too quickly!

"Now for the wedding plans!" Lobelia held up a list she had made. "The wedding shall take place in the rose garden," she said.

Mordred frowned. "What rose garden?"

"The one I shall plant in the castle yard," Lobelia replied. "I'm thinking red roses to go with the redhead theme. After the wedding, we'll have the feast. Frypot and I planned a menu to go with Belcheena's favorite letter— *W.* We're serving whitefish, Welsh rarebit, wolf chops, weasel tenderloin, wrens and warblers baked in a pie, watermelon, and wine. But Mordie, this will not come cheap."

"Spare no expense!" Mordred said. "A

princess must have a proper wedding. And surely Belcheena will pay for the whole shebang!"

Lobelia nodded. "Now, Wiglaf, you must pick a best man. Your most trusted friend in the world. One to stand by you as you say your vows."

"You should choose someone important," Mordred said. "Someone powerful. Someone...like me."

Wiglaf rolled his eyes. Mordred was the cause of this mess. He would never pick him. Angus and Erica were his good friends. But his most trusted friend in the world? That was his pig, Daisy. Wiglaf almost laughed, thinking what Mordred and Lobelia would say if he suggested that Daisy be in the wedding. A best pig! They would think he had lost his mind!

And suddenly Wiglaf realized that's just what he *would* say! If Mordred and Lobelia thought he was crazy, maybe they would give up trying to make him marry the princess.

"My best friend must stand by me!" Wiglaf declared.

"Fine," Lobelia said. "Just tell me his name. I will have him measured for a new tunic."

"It is a she," Wiglaf said. "My pig, Daisy."

"Your pig? Over my dead body!" Mordred roared.

"Daisy must stand by me!" Wiglaf smiled strangely. He tried to look quite mad.

"I'll roast that pig of yours for the wedding supper!" Mordred roared.

"Stop, Mordie," Lobelia said. "Clearly the pig cannot be the best man. But picture this. Daisy as...the flower girl!"

"Have you lost your mind?" Mordred bellowed.

"Not her, me!" Wiglaf cried. "I'm the one who's lost my mind!"

"Shush!" Lobelia said. "A flower pig has

never been done. It's new. Cutting-edge! What a statement it would make!"

Panic gripped Wiglaf. He had not counted on this! How could Lobelia want a pig in a wedding? He had to do something fast.

"Yes! Here's the statement it would make!" Wiglaf said. And he started oinking like a pig.

"Stop that, Wiglaf," ordered Lobelia. "It would say our lives are connected to the earth. To beasts—the pig. This is such a fine idea," she added. "Perhaps the hens should be in the wedding, too."

"Ooooh! I feel a headache coming on!" Mordred groaned. "All right, Lobelia. Make what plans you will. But I warn you..." He raised one bushy eyebrow. "Don't do a thing that will put a stop to this wedding. For I shall let nothing—*nothing!*—stand between me and that pot of gold!"

Chapter 4

Wiglaf stumbled into the dorm room late that night. But Angus and Erica had waited up for him.

"What happened, Wiggie?" Erica whispered. "Did you talk Mordred out of this crazy idea?"

Wiglaf shook his head. "Mordred wrote Belcheena that he had found the perfect husband for her.... Me!" he wailed. "Yorick is on his way to Mildew Palace with the letter right now!"

"Well, look at the bright side," Angus advised. "You will be very rich."

"What do I care for riches?" Wiglaf moaned.

"You can order the best suit of armor from *The Sir Lancelot Catalog*," Erica pointed out. "And the ruby-handled sword!"

Wiglaf pictured the handsome ruby-handled sword from Erica's catalog. That part didn't sound so bad.

"No more lumpen pudding," Angus said. "And no more Scrubbing Class!"

"I hadn't thought about that," Wiglaf said.

"And someone will wait on you, hand and foot," Erica added. "You'll like that, Wiggie."

Wiglaf smiled. "That's *Prince* Wiggie to you!" Then his smile faded. "But I don't want to get mar... Oh, why did Mordred write that letter?"

"You know..." Angus said thoughtfully. "We, too, can write a letter."

Erica grinned. "Our letter could say how awful Wiglaf of Pinwick really is!"

"Yes!" Wiglaf cried. "Let us write it now!"

Erica ran off to her bunk. She quickly returned with paper and a goose quill pen.

"You write it, Angus." She gave him the supplies. "You have the worst handwriting."

"All right," Angus agreed. He settled himself on the floor. "What shall I write?"

"Dear Princess Belcheena," Wiglaf began. "A greedy matchmaker wrote you of a red-headed dragon slayer, Wiglaf of Pinwick. He wrote that Wiglaf would make you a perfect husband. Nothing could be further from the truth!"

"Let me add a bit," Erica said. And she took over. "You will know Wiglaf when you see him by the handsome wart on the tip of his nose. His lips are always nicely moist, for his drooling keeps them wet. Are you fond of dogs? I ask, for Wiglaf's breath is so like that of a hound. His teeth are artistically arranged. Some lean to the left. Others to the right. Still others lean way out of his mouth."

"Enough about my looks," Wiglaf said quickly.

Erica nodded. "Wiglaf would rather walk a mile on burning coals than marry you," she went on. "But he is a fortune hunter. And you have a fortune. So he shall wed you for your gold." Erica smiled. "That is enough, I think."

Wiglaf took the pen. He signed the letter, "From a True Friend at DSA." He blew on the ink to dry it. Then he rolled the letter up. Erica tied it with a ribbon.

"Let us keep this mar...mar...this thing a secret," Wiglaf suggested. "I have no wish for the other students here to know about it."

"I shan't say a word," Angus promised.

"Me either," Erica said. "I swear it on my genuine Sir Lancelot sword!"

The three friends locked pinkies to seal their promise.

"Maybe Yorick is back from Mildew Palace by now," Erica said. "Let's go see."

They tiptoed out of the dorm. They ran

silently through the hallways and across the castle yard. Wiglaf opened the door to the gatehouse. But it was empty except for a large rock on a pile of straw.

"Too bad," Angus said. "Yorick isn't here."

Suddenly the rock sat up. A hand reached out and slipped off a gray hood.

"Yorick!" Wiglaf exclaimed. "We thought you were a rock."

"That's the idea," Yorick said, getting to his feet. "This is my rock disguise—gray tights, a gray tunic, gray hood. When I spot trouble, I squat down by the side of the road. People take me for a rock and walk on by."

"We have a letter, Yorick," Wiglaf said. "It must be delivered to Mildew Palace right away."

"I just got back from there!" Yorick exclaimed. "I'm not going again so soon. Not on your life."

"I shall pay you a penny," Angus offered.

"No, Angus!" Wiglaf cried. "Your mother gave you that penny for your birthday!"

"It's a small price to pay to keep you from getting married and— oops!" Angus clapped a hand to his mouth.

"Wiglaf's getting married?" Yorick asked.

"Not if I can help it," Wiglaf said quickly. "That's why we need you to take this letter."

Angus gave Yorick the penny. Yorick bit down on it to make sure it was real.

"I'm off!" Yorick took the letter from Wiglaf. He tucked it into his tunic. And he hurried away.

Tomorrow morning, Wiglaf thought, *Princess Belcheena will read this letter. And she will never want to lay eyes on Wiglaf of Pinwick!*

Wiglaf, Angus, and Erica started back across the yard. They had almost reached the castle when a voice called: "Halt! Who goes there?"

Wiglaf froze. So did Angus and Erica.

"Oh, it's you three," the voice said. It belonged to Coach Plungett. "I thought I'd caught a pack of thieves on my watch," Coach said with a chuckle. He put his sword away. "What are you lads doing out here at this time of night?"

"We...uh," Wiglaf began. "We were just..."

"We couldn't sleep," Erica put in.

"Couldn't sleep, eh?" Coach looked up at the starry sky. "I once suffered from sleepless nights," he said. "It was long ago. I couldn't sleep for thinking of my lady love."

"You were in love!" Angus cried. "Yuck!"

Wiglaf smiled. It was funny to think of Coach Plungett in love. And yet...Coach had never married. How had he escaped?

"Excuse me, Coach?" Wiglaf said. "If I may ask—how is it you never mar...mar..."

"Married?" Coach said. "I was a lowly squire and my lady love's father thought I'd never amount to a hill of beans. One night he sent his henchmen to tell me to go. Said they'd stab me full of holes if I returned. There were twenty of them. And only one of me. So I rode off. I thought it best at the time." Coach sighed. "But sometimes I wonder, lads."

Wiglaf sighed, too. Clearly Coach's story was no help to him.

"That's a sad tale, Coach," said Angus.

"'Tis," Coach agreed. "Now go in and get some sleep. I won't be in class for a few days, you know. I'm off to Ratswhiskers to visit my mother. Sir Mort will take over for me. He'll be showing you the Fatal Blow."

"Good night, Coach," the three called. Then they headed for the castle.

Wiglaf had a light heart all day on Thursday. He pictured the princess opening the second letter. And crossing Wiglaf of

Pinwick off her list of possible husbands.

Friday morning, Wiglaf, Erica, and Angus walked into the dining hall for breakfast. Wiglaf caught sight of Mordred. He was running toward him, waving a piece of parchment. The headmaster was smiling broadly. This was not a good sign.

"Princess Belcheena has written back!" Mordred exclaimed as he reached Wiglaf.

Wiglaf's heart began to pound. Something was amiss. He could feel it in his bones.

"Her steward brought her reply this morning," Mordred went on. "Listen to what she says!"

Wiglaf looked nervously around the dining hall. All the boys had stopped eating. They were silent, waiting to hear more.

"*My dear Mordred,*" Mordred read loudly. "*How kind of you to write to let me know that Wiglaf of Pinwick would make me such a fine husband!*"

"Woo! Woo! Woo!" shouted all the boys in the dining hall. "Wiglaf's getting married!"

"Silence!" Mordred roared. His violet eyes flashed with anger. He read on.

"'I shall gladly come to Dragon Slayers' Academy to meet this redheaded dragon slayer. Please have your best room ready for me.' Then she says something about even if I have to move out of the best room myself...clean sheets, blah, blah, blah. Let me see..." His eyes traveled down the page. "Ah! *I shall arrive on Saturday with my ladies-in-waiting, servants, and hangers-on. If Wiglaf is as perfect as you say, we shall be wed the following Saturday. I shall, of course, bring the pot of gold.*

Sincerely,

Princess Belcheena, Mildew Palace.'"

"Let us be wed, Wiglaf, honey!" called a boy.

Wiglaf's face burned hot with shame.

"She'll bring her gold!" Mordred exclaimed.

"That is the main thing. And she will be here tomorrow! Oh, there is much to do!"

Wiglaf tried to think. Belcheena must have sent this letter before she received the second one. Yes, that was it. Surely Mordred would soon get a second letter from Belcheena. And this one would say she was not coming after all.

"We must hurry!" Mordred said over the jeering boys. "We can't have Belcheena backing out of the deal when she lays eyes on you, Wiglaf. Come!" He grabbed Wiglaf's arm. "We must get you to Lobelia right away! She'll teach you manners. Show you how to eat with a knife, the way proper folks do. She'll show you how to bow. And most important, how to kiss the princess's hand."

The last thing Wiglaf heard as Mordred dragged him from the dining hall was boys making loud, juicy kissing sounds.

Chapter 5

"**S**ister!" Mordred cried. He flung Wiglaf into Lobelia's chamber. "Teach this riffraff some manners. And quickly! Belcheena is coming tomorrow. We can't have her refusing to marry the boy because he acts like a peasant."

"Tomorrow!" Lobelia gasped. "We don't have a moment to lose! Kneel down, Wiglaf. For you must kneel when you first speak to the princess."

Wiglaf fell to his knees.

"Start by praising Belcheena," Lobelia said. "Tell her she has lovely eyes and hair and lips. Make your bride-to-be feel beautiful!"

"Uh...beautiful Belcheena," Wiglaf began. "You have hair. And...uh, teeth..."

"Oh, for goodness' sakes!" Mordred cried. "Like this!" The big man dropped to his knees. He clasped his hands together. He blinked his violet eyes. "Oh, my lovely billionairess...er, I mean, princess!" he said. "Your hair shines like pure gold in the sunlight. Your eyes are as blue as sapphires! Your teeth are as bright as freshly minted coins!"

Wiglaf tried again. "Oh, Princess, your skin is as soft...as...as a sheep's belly."

"Not a sheep's belly!" Mordred bellowed.

"A sheep's belly *is* very soft," Wiglaf said.

"But not terribly romantic," Lobelia pointed out. "Say soft as a cloud."

After the praising lesson, Lobelia sat Wiglaf down. He practiced keeping his elbows off the table. He practiced drinking from a goblet without slurping. All the while, Lobelia read to him from *Medieval Manners: Do's and Don't's.*

"'Don't spit in your plate during dinner,'"

she read. "'Wait until the meal is finished. Don't pick your teeth with your knife—always use the point of your sword. Don't blow your nose on the hem of the tablecloth. Use your sleeve.'"

Lobelia kept at it all morning. She dismissed Wiglaf for lunch, telling him to practice his manners in the dining hall. Wiglaf's head spun with do's and don't's as he carried his tray to the Class I table.

"Wiglaf!" Erica exclaimed as he sat down. "I have good news!"

"What?" Wiglaf's heart leapt with hope. "Has Yorick returned with an answer from Belcheena?"

"No. But my order from *The Sir Lancelot Catalog* came!" Erica announced.

Wiglaf's heart sank. "That's nice," he managed.

"Here," Erica said. "I want you to have this." She pressed a ring into his hand. It had a milky blue stone. "It's a Sir Lancelot almost-magic foretelling ring," she explained. "When the stone is blue, all is well. But if it turns orange and starts blinking, it means *danger, danger, danger!*"

Wiglaf slipped the ring onto the first finger of his left hand. The stone's blue glow comforted him somehow. He thanked Erica.

"After lunch, let's go find Yorick," Angus suggested. "Maybe he has brought back Belcheena's reply. And surely that will be good news."

They found Yorick outside the henhouse. He was gathering feathers for his pigeon disguise.

"Yorick!" Wiglaf called. "Did you give Princess Belcheena the letter?"

"Uh...thieves set upon me!" Yorick cried.

"Didn't you squat down on the side of the road and pretend to be a rock?" Angus asked.

"Of course I did!" Yorick said. "But the

thieves thought I *was* a rock. So they sat on me! I let out a cry. And the next thing I knew, they were robbing me! Took my penny, they did. So here." Yorick pulled the letter from his tunic and gave it to Wiglaf. "I knew you wouldn't want me delivering it without my proper pay."

Wiglaf groaned. Here was his last chance to keep Belcheena from coming to DSA—ruined! He crumpled the letter into a ball.

Erica patted Wiglaf on the back. "Don't worry, Wiggie," she said. "Look. Your ring is still blue. There is no danger. Everything will turn out all right. Come! Let us be off to Slaying Class. Sir Mort is teaching us today."

"I shall be there in a minute," Wiglaf told his friends. "First I must go see Daisy."

Wiglaf walked to the henhouse.

"Daisy?" he called. "Are you here, girl?"

Daisy came trotting out to meet Wiglaf.

"Ello-hay, Iggie-way!" she exclaimed.

Wiglaf knelt down. He put his arms around his pig and hugged her.

"I can't stay long, Daisy," he said. "But I had to see you. For alas! Mordred is trying to make me get mar...mar..." No sound came out. But he managed to mouth the word.

Daisy gasped. "Arried-may?"

Wiglaf nodded. Then he poured his heart out to his pig. "I even tried to get out of it by saying that you must be in the wedding," Wiglaf added.

"Eally-ray?" Daisy said brightly.

Wiglaf nodded. "But Lobelia liked the idea! She wants you to be the flower pig!"

"I-yay ould-way ove-lay o-tay!" Daisy said.

"No, no!" Wiglaf cried. "I don't want to get mar... I want things to stay just as they are!"

"Illy-say oy-bay!" Daisy exclaimed. "I-yay ove-lay eddings-way!"

Wiglaf moaned. Daisy didn't seem to understand. He had counted on his wise pig to help him. He had never guessed that Daisy was so very fond of weddings.

"E-may, a-yay ower-flay ig-pay!" Daisy burbled happily. "Is-thay is-yay e-thay appiest-hay ay-day of-yay y-may ife-lay!"

"I must go to Slaying, Daisy." Wiglaf stood up. He rubbed his pig on her head. Then he stumbled from the henhouse in a daze.

Slaying Class went badly for Wiglaf that afternoon. He was late, for one thing. And he never had gotten the homework from Torblad. Sir Mort called on him to name three spots on a dragon where a dragon slayer could strike a fatal blow. But he could not name even one. The old knight looked very disappointed.

When at last class ended, Wiglaf ran over to Angus and Erica.

"I have an idea," he whispered to them. "For getting out of getting mar...mar... For getting out of this mess. I shall call Zelnoc!"

"That crazy wizard?" Angus asked. "The one who messed up Daisy's speech spell?"

"He's not very good," Wiglaf admitted. "But he *is* a wizard. Surely he must have some magic that can help me."

"We have a break before Alchemy Class," Erica said. "Let us summon this enchanter now."

"I know a secret part of the dungeon," Angus added. "No one ever goes there."

"Perfect," Wiglaf said. "Let's go there now. For my time is running out!"

Chapter 6

Wiglaf, Angus, and Erica ran down the stone stairway to the dungeon. Angus led them to a damp room way at the back. A tiny window near the ceiling let in the only light.

Wiglaf closed his eyes. He chanted Zelnoc's name backwards three times: "Conlez, Conlez, Conlez."

A faint breeze tickled Wiglaf's cheek. He opened his eyes. A puff of smoke was rising from the floor. The puff grew and grew until the room was filled with thick black smoke.

Wiglaf's eyes began to water.

Angus and Erica started coughing.

Then suddenly, out of the smoke, leapt a

white rabbit. It was followed by another. And another. Before long, dozens of the furry creatures were hopping around the dungeon.

"Zelnoc?" Wiglaf called. "Are you here?"

"Of course I am!" boomed a voice inside the smoke. "I was summoned, was I not?"

With that, the smoke lifted. And there stood a wizard. He wore a dark blue pointed hat and robe, dotted with silver stars.

"Whoa!" Angus said. He and Erica backed up.

Zelnoc stepped forward, tripping over a rabbit.

"Blasted bunnies!" he cursed. "How was I to know that saying *Bibbity Babbit* summoned rabbits? I thought I was doing a wart removal chant. So, it's you, is it, Weglip?"

"Yes, sir." Wiglaf began to worry. He had forgotten how mixed up Zelnoc's spells could get. "These are my friends, Eric and Angus."

"Charmed," Zelnoc said. "Do either of you know a spell for getting rid of rabbits?"

Erica and Angus shook their heads.

"I didn't think so," Zelnoc said miserably. He turned to Wiglaf. "So, what'll it be this time, Wigloaf? Another courage spell?"

"No, sir," Wiglaf said. "I need a spell so I won't have to get mar...mar..."

"Married," Angus put in. "My Uncle Mordred is arranging for him to marry Princess Belcheena."

"A princess, eh?" Zelnoc exclaimed. "Good work, my boy! Princesses don't usually go for you peasant types."

"I don't want her to go for me," Wiglaf exclaimed. "I called you to get me out of it!"

"No problem," Zelnoc said. "I'll brew you an anti-love potion. Belcheena takes a few sips of it and—zowie! The first person she lays eyes on, she shall hate with all her might."

"That sounds perfect!" Wiglaf said. "And I shall make certain that person is *me!*"

"Tell me, wizard," Erica said. "What do you put into such a potion?"

"A pinch of pepper, six hairs from a skunk tail, a lump of lumpen pudding," Zelnoc said. "I can't tell the whole recipe, of course. That would be breaking Wizard Rule #457. But it's a doozie."

"When can I have it?" Wiglaf asked.

"Let me think...." The wizard tapped his fingers on his chin. "Two weeks from today."

"Alas!" Wiglaf cried. "Then I am doomed!"

"The wedding is to take place next Saturday," Angus explained.

"Why didn't you say it was a rush job?" asked Zelnoc. "Nothing is impossible! We wizards always have a trick up our sleeves!"

To prove his point, Zelnoc reached up his sleeve. He pulled out...a rabbit.

"Egad!" he cried as the bunny jumped from his hand. "I'm having a really bad hare day!"

"Is there nothing else you can do for Wiglaf, sir?" asked Erica.

"There is always something else," Zelnoc said. "I'll give Waglom a smelling spell. It's like perfume—with a kick. Let me see…. Ah! I know! Whiff of Loathing. That's the ticket. One sniff, and bingo! Belcheena will detest you forever! Or at least until the spell wears off. Never fear! I shall bring it soon. Now, I must get back to my tower and figure out how to get rid of these rabbits."

"Oh, thank you, sir!" Wiglaf said, as, once more, the dungeon filled with smoke.

"Farewell, Wugloom!" Zelnoc called. "Come, bunnies! Hop to it!"

The rabbits jumped into the smoke with Zelnoc. Then, one and all, they disappeared.

Wiglaf ran happily up the dungeon stairs after Erica and Angus. Summoning Zelnoc had been a good idea after all! At the top of the stairs, they bumped into Mordred.

"Wiglaf!" the headmaster boomed. "I've been looking for you." He sniffed. "Do I smell smoke?"

"Frypot must have burned the lumpen pudding again," Angus said quickly.

"Ah, yes," Mordred said. "Come, Wiglaf! Lobelia is waiting!"

"But sir!" Wiglaf said. "I have to go to Alchemy Class."

"Classes are canceled," Mordred said. "Except for Scrubbing. Eric and Angus, you missed the sign-up. So you'll have to scrub the privy. Wiglaf, you go to Lobelia's. She's waiting to give you a makeover."

"A...what?" Wiglaf said.

"Lobelia wants you to look your best when you meet Belcheena tomorrow," Mordred said. "So go!"

Wiglaf hurried down the hallway. To his

horror, he saw that the stone in his ring was turning orange. It started blinking: *danger, danger, danger!* His heart pounded. This was not a good sign.

"Wiglaf!" Lobelia exclaimed as she waved him into her chamber. "I found the most charming drawing of Prince Putroc in *Royal Lads Magazine*. Just feast your eyes on his hair!" Lobelia held up the drawing. Prince Putroc's hair hung down on his forehead in ringlet curls. "You, Wiglaf, will look royal when I've curled your hair."

"*My* hair?" Wiglaf cried. No wonder his ring had been blinking! "No! Please! That picture is...awful!"

"Trust me on this, Wiglaf," Lobelia said. "Those curls are *you!* But we have a few other things to take care of first. Sit on that stool."

Wiglaf sat. Lobelia began spreading foul-smelling green goo all over his face.

"This clay is from Dead Fish Swamp. It does wonders for the skin. There." She stepped back to see if she had missed any spots.

Wiglaf felt the clay hardening.

"Now tilt your head back," Lobelia said.

Wiglaf did as he was told.

"Cucumbers take away puffiness." She pressed two big slices over his eyes.

Wiglaf felt the juice trickling into his ears.

"And for your lips," Lobelia added, "pepper paste." She smeared some on.

"Yow!" Wiglaf yelped. "It stings!"

"That's what brings out the nice rosy color," Lobelia explained. "Try not to lick your lips."

Wiglaf wanted to ask how long he must have all this disgusting stuff on him. But he was afraid to open his mouth.

"You know your ears stick out, don't you, Wiglaf?" Lobelia went on. "Well, I'm told that half an onion will draw the ear closer to the head." She hung half an onion from a string on each of Wiglaf's ears.

"Now hold still while I work on your fingernails," Lobelia said. "Rough hands are the sign of a peasant. Maybe you should wear gloves."

When she finished his nails, Lobelia began wrapping strands of Wiglaf's hair around a red-hot curling iron.

Wiglaf had faced two fire-breathing dragons. They had not killed him. But he thought Lobelia might. Certainly she was skilled at torture.

It seemed to Wiglaf that his makeover took forever. But at last he found his way back to the dorm room. He had a nasty rash on his cheeks from the swamp clay. His lips burned a fiery red. Carrot-colored ringlets danced on his forehead.

"Wiglaf!" Erica exclaimed when she saw him. "Have you caught the plague?"

"I wish," Wiglaf moaned. "Death by plague must be better than a makeover!" He flopped down on his cot. "And the worst is yet to come. Belcheena arrives tomorrow."

"We have to help him, Angus," Erica said.

"We do," Angus agreed. "But how?"

"How indeed." Erica tapped her foot as she thought. "I do have one idea," she said at last. "The Bag-o-Laughs Kit I ordered from *Junior Jester Magazine*. That should do the trick!"

"Oh, I think I saw some of the stuff you got...like the flower that squirts water?" Angus said. "And the black gum that makes one's teeth appear to be missing? And the hand buzzer? And the fake doggie poo?"

"Yes!" Erica answered with a smile. "We shall give Belcheena a very special welcome indeed!"

Chapter 7

On Saturday morning, Wiglaf opened his eyes. He checked his ring. It was blue now. But surely it would soon turn orange. For this was the day Belcheena was coming!

After breakfast, Wiglaf slowly made his way to Lobelia's chamber. He had just raised his hand to knock on the door, when a bright light flashed before him.

"Egad!" cried Wiglaf, jumping back.

In the spot where the light had been, Zelnoc shimmered into being.

"How do you like my new entrance?" the wizard asked. "I call it 'The Flash.' Beats the smoke, yes sir! I'm on a roll now, Waglop! I invented Bunnies-B-Gone. And poof! No more rabbits!"

"That's nice," Wiglaf said. "Did you bring me the loathing stuff?"

"Do bats have wings?" the wizard said. "Of course I did!" He reached up his sleeve and pulled out a bottle of bright red liquid.

"Are you sure it will work?" Wiglaf asked.

Zelnoc scowled down at Wiglaf. "Would I bring you something that didn't work?"

"Well..." Wiglaf didn't know how to put it. Zelnoc's spells had a way of turning out badly.

Just then, Lobelia opened her door.

"Hello, Wiglaf," she said. Then she looked at Zelnoc. "A wizard!" she exclaimed. "But why are you dressed in that old robe?"

Zelnoc frowned. "What's wrong with it?"

"That star pattern is *so* last year," Lobelia said. "Wizards nowadays go in for comets, meteor showers, shooting stars. They want a powerful image. But come in, both of you." She smiled. "I have a surprise for Wiglaf."

A surprise? Wiglaf had had more than enough of those. But he followed Zelnoc into Lobelia's chamber. And there was Daisy.

Wiglaf stared. His pig wore a pink silk cape. A crown of tiny rosebuds sat on her head.

"Why are you dressed up?" Zelnoc asked.

"Iglaf-way's edding-way," Daisy said.

"Ah, yes. The wedding." Zelnoc winked at Wiglaf. "That's why I'm here, too, in a way."

Lobelia gasped. "Wiglaf, that's brilliant!" she cried. "A wizard in your wedding!"

"No, no, no," Zelnoc said. "Wizard Rule #45 clearly states *no wizards in weddings*. Funerals, sometimes. But weddings? Never."

"Oh, rules were made to be broken," Lobelia scoffed. She began circling Zelnoc. "I'll trim your beard and find you a new robe. One that will make you *look* powerful, even if your powers aren't up to scratch."

"What?" Zelnoc cried. "My powers are just fine, thank you very much."

"Don't get huffy," Lobelia said.

"Huffy?" Zelnoc exclaimed. "Wizards don't get huffy! Wizards get *angry!* Wizards get *even!* Especially mighty, powerful wizards, like me!"

"Oh, puh-leeze!" Lobelia exclaimed.

Zelnoc reached up his sleeve and pulled out the red potion. He popped the cork.

"Doubt my powers, will you?" Zelnoc snarled. "Well, let's have a little test."

He waved the bottle under Lobelia's nose.

Wiglaf watched in horror as Lobelia's violet eyes began rolling around in circles.

"What have you done?" Wiglaf cried.

Lobelia's eyes closed. Then they popped open. Lobelia stared at Zelnoc.

"Well?" the wizard said eagerly. "You hate me with all your heart, don't you?"

She clasped her hands to her chest and cried,

"Oh, say not such a cruel thing!
With love for you my heart does sing!"

"Uh-oh," said Zelnoc.

Lobelia went on:

"Your wizard's hat is such a tall one!
In love with you I must have fallen!"

"E-shay oves-lay ou-yay!" Daisy sang happily.

"This is worse than rabbits!" Zelnoc cried.

Lobelia continued:

"Oh, Wizard, though you're old and wrinkled,
With love for you my heart is sprinkled!"

Wiglaf grabbed the bottle of red liquid from Zelnoc's hand. He read the tiny printing on the label: "Oil of Rhymes-o-Love."

"Oops," Zelnoc said. "I picked up the wrong bottle. But it works, Wuglop. You can see that, can't you? My spells do work!"

Lobelia took Zelnoc's hand in hers.

"Wizard, with your beard so white!
Dance with me in the pale moonlight!"

Zelnoc pulled his hand away. "Wizard Rule #498—*no dancing*. I'm getting out of here!"

Lobelia cried,

"Oh, wizard, with your robe so blue,

If you leave, I'll cry: Boo hoo!"

Zelnoc turned to Wiglaf. "I'm gone," he said. And with a bright flash of light, he was.

Tears streamed down Lobelia's cheeks.

"My wizard, he is gone from me.

I cannot stand such misery!"

"You don't really love him, my lady," Wiglaf said weakly. "It's a spell. It will wear off."

But Lobelia would not be comforted. She cried and sobbed and carried on. At last she threw her velvet cloak around her shoulders.

"Where are you going?" Wiglaf asked.

Lobelia cried miserably:

"This pain I feel, I must be stopping!

There's just one cure—I'm going shopping!"

Chapter 8

Wiglaf sank onto Lobelia's couch. He should have known better than to call Zelnoc. Whiff of Loathing indeed!

"Oor-pay Obelia-lay!" Daisy exclaimed.

"Lobelia's spell will wear off," Wiglaf said. "But Belcheena will be mine forever!"

Mordred stuck his head in the door.

"Ah, here you are, Wiglaf!" he exclaimed. "Yorick has just spotted Princess Belcheena! She and her party are starting up Huntsman's Path. They will be here within the hour!"

"Woe is me!" Wiglaf groaned.

"Why are you not dressed?" Mordred asked. "And where is my sister?"

"Opping-shay," Daisy said.

"Shopping?" Mordred cried. "At a time like this? She must have gotten wind of that bodice sale over in Ratswhiskers. Well, never mind. Now where did she put that new outfit she ordered for you, Wiglaf? Ah, here it is!" Mordred picked up a package tied up with string. He thrust it into Wiglaf's hands.

Instantly, Wiglaf's ring begin to flash a bright orange warning.

"Go put it on!" Mordred roared.

Wiglaf shook as he ducked behind the tapestry. He was in danger! But what could he do? He took off his DSA uniform. He put on his new outfit.

"Don't dillydally, boy!" Mordred yelled.

Wiglaf quickly fastened the squirting flower that Erica had given him to the collar of his new tunic. He stuck the tooth-black gum into his pocket. He slipped the hand buzzer onto his palm. Then he stepped out from behind the tapestry.

Wiglaf yelped as he beheld himself in Lobelia's looking glass. No wonder his ring had signaled danger! For he wore a swamp-green velvet tunic. His skinny legs, in matching tights, looked like swamp-green toothpicks. His shoes had long, curled-up toes!

Mordred set a swamp-green mushroom-shaped hat on top of Wiglaf's ringlets. "There!" he said. "The hat gives you a lordly look."

"Ery-vay oble-nay!" Daisy exclaimed.

Wiglaf didn't think "noble" was quite the right word. The right word was "ninny." He looked like some half-witted elf!

Wiglaf stared at himself. And then he smiled. Surely Princess Belcheena would never marry anyone who looked this foolish!

"Come!" Mordred said. "It is time for you to go to the castle yard to greet your bride!"

Wiglaf's shoes flapped as he followed Mordred outside.

Every DSA student stood in the castle yard, waiting to see the East Armpittsian princess.

Wiglaf heard giggles as he passed by.

"Look at mushroom head!" called a boy.

"Hey, string bean legs!" called another.

But Wiglaf walked with his head held high. So what if they laughed? If the silly outfit saved him from marrying Belcheena, he would gladly wear it for the rest of his life.

Wiglaf spotted Angus and Erica in the crowd. But he could only wave to them and walk on.

Suddenly trumpets sounded. And Yorick cried, "Her Royal Highness, Princess Belcheena!"

Then through the castle gates marched a juggler juggling oranges. He was followed by two jesters turning cartwheels. Three minstrels strolled in next, strumming their lutes and singing. Four ladies-in-waiting were followed by five servants. The last one held the leash of a fierce-looking wild boar with golden tips on his tusks.

Wiglaf had never seen such a glorious parade. If only he did not know who was at the end of it.

Now a team of six horses pulled a golden carriage through the gate. And waving from the window was none other than Princess Belcheena.

"Welcome to Dragon Slayers' Academy!" Mordred boomed. He nodded to the DSA band. The boys struck up a squeaky tune.

Wiglaf watched with growing dread as the servants opened the carriage door. The ladies-in-waiting helped Princess Belcheena out.

Belcheena was a large princess. Much larger than Wiglaf had expected. A pointed hat sat on her head. A long lacy scarf trailed down from its tip. Her braided yellow hair hung down nearly to her knees.

"Welcome, Princess!" Mordred said. "As headmaster of this fine academy, I welcome—"

"Stop!" Princess Belcheena cried.

Mordred stopped midspeech.

"Well, where is he?" the princess said loudly. "Where is this Wiglaf of Pinwick?"

"Right here, your loadedness!" Mordred said. "I mean, your loveliness! Go on, boy!" He gave Wiglaf a push. "Do as I taught you."

Wiglaf lurched forward.

"Look, Gretta," Belcheena said to the lady-in-waiting at her side. "His hair is not really red at all. I would call it orange."

Yes! Wiglaf thought. Belcheena wanted a truly redheaded husband. And he did not fill the bill!

"It is indeed orange," Wiglaf agreed.

To his surprise, the princess smiled. "My long-lost love had red-orange hair," she said. She plucked up a locket she wore on a chain around her neck. She opened it and sighed. "This is all I have left of him. A curl of his carroty hair!"

Wiglaf's face fell. This was not working out at all. She liked his stupid hair! But he wasn't giving up yet.

"Go on, Wiglaf. Compliment her," Mordred whispered.

Wiglaf stepped toward the princess.

"Beautiful Belcheena," he said. "You smell as sweet as the flower I wear on my tunic!"

Belcheena leaned forward to smell the flower. Wiglaf pushed a little bulb in his pocket. *Spuuuurt!* The flower squirted Belcheena's face.

"Aaack!" cried the surprised princess.

"My lady!" screamed Gretta. She began patting Belcheena's cheeks dry with her handkerchief.

Before the princess could recover, Wiglaf struck again. "Princess Belcheena," he said. "Let me kiss your hand!"

He took Belcheena's hand in his and squeezed.

The hand buzzer sounded: *Buzzzzzzzzzz!*

"Yowie!" Belcheena cried. She jumped back.

Mordred rushed over to Belcheena.

"Princess!" he cried. "I shall have Wiglaf flogged! I'll put him in the Thumb Screws. I'll put him in the Foot Smasher. I'll put him in the Limb Stretcher until his arms are six feet long!"

"Shush!" Belcheena waved Mordred away. She eyed Wiglaf. "I was not expecting that!" she said.

Wiglaf smiled broadly.

"Please forgive Wiglaf, Princess!" Mordred cried. "I shall throw him in the dungeon! But of course, you will still marry him, won't you? You'll still give me that great big pot of gold?"

"Scat!" Belcheena yelled at Mordred.

The headmaster slunk away.

"Tell me, Wiglaf of Pinwick!" Belcheena said. "The squirting flower and the hand buzzer...are they from the Junior Jester Bag-o-Laughs Kit?"

The question caught Wiglaf by surprise.

"Why, yes, they are, my lady," he answered.

"Ha!" Belcheena cried. She gave Wiglaf a hearty slap on the back. "There's nothing I like better than a practical joke!" She grinned. "I, too, ordered the Bag-o-Laughs! I was going to have some fun with you! Just look!"

Belcheena slipped her hand into the pocket of her gown. She brought her hand to her mouth. Then she smiled, and her two front teeth appeared to be missing.

Belcheena threw back her head and roared with laughter. She gave Wiglaf another mighty slap. This one sent him sprawling face-down in the castle yard.

"You are not half the man my long-lost love was," the princess said as Wiglaf struggled to his feet. "Not even a quarter, really. But you're a rascal! Oh, what fine times we shall have at Mildew Palace!"

"You...you like him then?" Mordred asked. "You still want to marry Wiglaf?"

"Why not?" Belcheena boomed. "And why wait a week? Let us be wed tomorrow!"

"But...but...but..." Wiglaf sputtered.

He was drowned out by Mordred. "Oh, joy! Oh, golden day!" the headmaster cried. "By the way, your royal richness. I mean, highness...about that pot of gold."

Princess Belcheena rolled her eyes. "Is that all you can think of?" she asked.

"Well, frankly...yes," Mordred mumbled. "I mean, no! Of course not!"

"Good," said the princess. "Now, I have had

a hard journey to this forsaken part of the kingdom. I want to rest. Is your very best room ready for me?"

"Yes, Princess!" Mordred said. "Yorick!" he called. "Show the princess to her room!"

"Ta ta, Wigs!" Belcheena wiggled her fingers at him. "Wait! What is that on your head?"

"What?" said Wiglaf. He swatted at his hair.

"This." Belcheena reached out and seemed to pluck something from the top of his head. She held it out in front of him.

It was a...a human thumb! Blood was caked around its base where it had been cut from a hand! Wiglaf swayed dizzily, just looking at it.

"Ha!" Belcheena cackled. "Gotcha, Wigs!"

She tossed the horrid thumb to him. It was made of rubber. Then she skipped merrily into the castle.

"Back to class, boys!" Mordred cried. "We'll celebrate tonight at Wiglaf's bachelor party!"

"Hooray!" the students cheered.

Angus and Erica ran over to Wiglaf. "I'm doomed!" Wiglaf cried.

"No, you're not," Erica said. "Look at your ring. The stone is still blue."

But Wiglaf was losing faith in his ring. "Here," he said, handing the thumb to Erica.

"Thanks!" Erica exclaimed. "The severed thumb only comes in the super-duper Bag-o-Laughs. You get a whoopie cushion with that one, too."

"That's nice," said Wiglaf. But he wasn't thinking about whoopie cushions. Or severed thumbs. He was thinking of Princess Belcheena. And how he was going to be spending the rest of his life with her.

Chapter 9

"Three cheers for the groom!" Mordred boomed as Wiglaf walked into the dining hall for his bachelor party that night.

"Hip, hip, hooray!" everyone cried three times.

The room was hung with greenery. Platters of steaming food lined the tables. There wasn't a bowl of lumpen pudding in sight.

Wiglaf sat in the seat of honor. Angus and Erica sat on either side of him. They dug into the dinner. But Wiglaf could not eat a bite.

Mordred strolled by. "Eat up, Wiglaf!" he roared. "I've spared no expense. Ah, what fun it is to spend the princess's money!" He clapped

Wiglaf on the back. "Have you picked a best man yet, my boy?"

Wiglaf turned to Angus. "Would you?" he asked.

"Honored," Angus said, with his mouth full.

During dinner, the juggler juggled. The minstrels sang. The boar was led around the room so that all might admire his fine gold-tipped tusks. Wiglaf would have enjoyed himself tremendously if only there had been another reason for the party.

Coach Plungett stood up to give a toast. He raised his flask. "Word reached me at my mother's cottage in Ratswhiskers that you were getting married, Wiglaf," he said. "I rushed back to wish you all the happiness in the world! Love is a wonderful thing, lad. Why, thinking of my long-lost lady love still makes my heart beat with joy. Some would say that I have been unlucky in love. Yet I say—not so! For a while, my lady love and I were as happy as pigs in a mud wallow. I remember the time..."

"Give your toast and sit down, Wendell!" Frypot called. "We don't want to be here all night!"

"To Wiglaf and his bride!" Coach said.

"Here! Here!" everyone shouted. "To Wiglaf and Belcheena!"

"Belcheena?" Suddenly, Coach choked on his mead and started coughing. Mordred had to slap him on the back for quite a while before the big man recovered.

Brother Dave gave the last toast of the evening. "Sleep well tonight, Wiglaf," the monk said. "For tomorrow when thou hearest wedding bells, they shall be ringing for thee!"

"I...I do," Wiglaf stuttered. He stood just

inside the door of the DSA castle, between his best man Angus and Mordred.

"Louder!" Mordred barked.

"I do!" Wiglaf shouted miserably.

Angus patted his shoulder.

The wedding was about to begin. Wiglaf pulled the scratchy pleated white collar away from his neck. Why did he have to wear the silly thing? Wasn't he in enough pain already?

A wedding day was supposed to be a happy day. But Wiglaf felt like crying. He did not want to leave his friends. He did not want to live in Mildew Palace with that prankster Belcheena. He did not even want to help her spend her billions.

"Once more," Mordred commanded.

"I dooooo!" wailed Wiglaf.

"That's better!" Mordred said.

Suddenly Lobelia rushed into the castle. She was loaded down with shopping bags.

"Oh, thank goodness!" she cried. "I made it back in time. I don't know what came over me, rushing off like that. Mordie, go check on Dr. Pluck. Tell him to start playing the organ!"

Mordred hurried off.

Lobelia uncapped a bottle from one of her bags. She squirted a sweet-smelling liquid on Wiglaf. "It's Groom Perfume," she said. "Isn't it wild? I'd better check on the bridesmaids now. I'll be back." And off she rushed.

Yuck! Now Wiglaf smelled just like a rose! He peeked out the door at Lobelia's rosebushes. They were in full bloom. A cloth runner had been put down on the grass for Belcheena to walk on. Class III students were seating the wedding guests on long wooden benches.

Suddenly organ music started playing. Yikes! The wedding had begun!

Brother Dave walked out of the chapel. He stopped between the two biggest rosebushes.

"That is our signal," Angus whispered.

Wiglaf stood rooted to the spot.

"Come on!" Angus said. And he pulled the reluctant groom out into the castle yard.

Wiglaf blinked in the sunlight. He walked toward Brother Dave.

"Thou art doing fine, lad," the monk said when Wiglaf reached him.

Next came the wedding party, Gretta and the other ladies-in-waiting, with Daisy trotting behind them. She was wearing her pink silk cape. And her crown of rosebuds.

People gasped when they saw Daisy. They murmured to each other "Pig in a wedding!" and "What next?"

Now Dr. Pluck pounded on the organ keys and struck up "Here Comes the Bride."

Sir Mort began escorting Belcheena up the

runner. The princess wore a red gown. Her yellow hair was done in two large horns that were wound with ropes of pearls.

"So beautiful!" whispered the wedding guests. "Such a lovely dress!"

Wiglaf swallowed as the princess walked closer and closer to him. Her lips were bright pink. Her cheeks were rouged red. Blue shadow lined her eyelids. Wiglaf thought she looked scarier than any dragon.

Wiglaf found Erica's face in the crowd. She held up a finger. Wiglaf understood. He looked down at his ring. The stone was bright blue.

Phooey! he thought. The thing ought to be glowing like a red-hot coal! Clearly, *The Sir Lancelot Catalog* had sold Erica a dud.

Sir Mort walked Belcheena to her groom. He put the princess's arm on Wiglaf's. Then he bowed and took a seat in the front row beside Mordred.

Belcheena winked and smiled at Wiglaf.

Wiglaf tried to smile back.

"Dearly beloved," Brother Dave began. "We have come here today to join Belcheena Kristen Louise Wilhemina Bernadette Paula Frieda Marie, Princess of East Armpittsia and Wiglaf of Pinwick in marriage."

Wiglaf's knees began to shake.

"Steady, Wiglaf," Angus whispered.

"If any persons here know of a reason why these two people should not be joined in marriage," Brother Dave went on, "let them speak now, or forever hold their peace."

Silence filled the castle yard.

Brother Dave turned to Belcheena.

"Princess Belcheena," he said. "Do you take this—"

"Stop!" called a voice from the gatehouse. "Stop the wedding now!"

Chapter 10

The wedding guests gasped.

Wiglaf whirled around. His eyes searched the crowd.

"Look, there." Angus pointed toward the gatehouse. A tall man was making his way through the crowd.

Wiglaf gasped. "It's Coach Plungett!"

What is going on? he wondered.

Suddenly Belcheena let out a scream.

Wiglaf jumped.

Was this another one of Belcheena's jokes?

"Wendell!" Belcheena called. "Is it you?"

"Yes, Belchie? It is!" Coach Plungett cried. He ran up to the princess. Belcheena slowly held out her hand. Coach reached for it. But the princess quickly drew her hand away. "Gotcha!" she shrieked.

"Whoo-whoo!" Coach Plungett cried. "It's my rowdy old Belchie!" Then he picked her up and whirled her around and around.

"STOP THAT!" Mordred boomed.

Coach put the princess down.

"What, in the name of King Ken's britches, are you doing, Plungett?" Mordred roared.

"Gazing at my long-lost love," Coach replied. "Dearest Belchie!" he said. "I thought never to see you again!"

"Why did you leave me, Wendell? Why?" Belcheena asked.

"Your father's henchmen drove me from your palace," Coach Plungett said. "Many times I tried to return. But the guards kept me out. At last I went off questing in the Dark Forest. I tried to forget you, Belchie. But I never could."

"I never forgot you either," Belcheena said. "After you left, all I did was count my gold, order silly things from *Junior Jester Magazine*, and sing this song. Listen." And Belcheena began to sing.

> *"He set my heart on fire,*
> *That's the truth, I am no liar.*
> *When he left I was a crier*
> *For the Squire of My Desire!*

> *"Throughout the whole empire*
> *He's the one that I admire.*
> *There is no squire higher*
> *Than the Squire of My Desire!"*

"Oh, Belchie!" cried Coach.

"Sit down, Plungett," Mordred ordered. "You and Belcheena can talk about old times later. Now, let's get back to the wedding!"

But the princess and the coach paid no attention to the headmaster.

"I shall not lose you again, Belchie!" Coach Plungett vowed. He dropped to his knees and said, "Will you marry me?"

The princess smiled. She turned to Wiglaf. "I hope you don't mind terribly," she said, "but I must marry Wendell."

"So you must, Princess," Wiglaf said happily. "You must marry the one you love."

There. He'd said it: Marry!

"What will your father say?" Coach asked.

"Who cares?" the princess replied.

"Hold it! Hold it!" Mordred cried. "What about your conditions, Your Highness? True, Wendell Plungett is a dragon slayer. And his first name begins with *W*. But," Mordred added slyly, "he does not have red hair!"

"'Tis true," Coach Plungett said. He pulled off his wig. "I no longer have *any* hair."

"Who cares?" Princess Belcheena said again. "You once had lovely carrot-colored hair. I still carry a curl of it in my locket. That is enough for me."

Mordred groaned.

"I'll be your best man, Coach," Wiglaf offered.

Brother Dave began again. "Dearly beloved, we have come here today to join Princess Belcheena of Mildew Palace, East Armpittsia, and Wendell Plungett of Dragon Slayers' Academy in marriage."

What a celebration followed! No one had a better time than Wiglaf. He cheered for the jugglers. He sang along with the minstrels. He danced with Daisy. Later he smiled when he saw his pig in the crowd, flirting with the golden-tusked boar. He'd never been so happy.

"Look," said Angus at last. "The bride and groom are getting into the carriage."

"Let us bid them good-bye," Erica said.

Wiglaf, Angus, and Erica hurried over.

"Farewell, Coach!" Wiglaf said. "Farewell, Princess Belcheena!"

"Good-bye!" Belcheena called. "Come and visit us at Mildew Palace, won't you, Wigs? And bring your friends."

Mordred pushed his way to the carriage. "Excuse me, Princess," he said. "But as your matchmaker, I was wondering.... About that pot of gold?"

"Ah!" Belcheena said. "But I have not married Wiglaf of Pinwick. So I owe you no pot of gold."

"But...but...but..." Mordred sputtered. "The price of the wedding supper alone..."

The princess reached out of the carriage and patted Mordred on the head. "Thanks for everything!" she exclaimed. Then the happy couple galloped off for their honeymoon.

"I'm ruined!" Mordred bellowed. "Ruined!"

He turned to Wiglaf, his violet eyes bulging. "It's all your fault!" he growled.

"*My* fault?" Wiglaf cried.

"If you weren't a redheaded dragon slayer named Wiglaf, none of this would have happened!" Mordred yelled. "I'm going to throw you into the dungeon. It's the Thumb Screws for you, my boy...."

The Sir Lancelot almost-magic ring began flashing a bright orange warning: *Danger, danger, danger!* Wiglaf didn't wait around to hear any more. He took off running. Angus and Erica took off after him. They knew just where to hide from Mordred until his temper cooled down—in the DSA library.

As Wiglaf ran, he felt better than he had felt in a long, long time. He felt as if he really might live happily ever after.

Find out what new adventures await our hero in:

Dragon Slayers' Academy 5

KNIGHT FOR A DAY

When Wiglaf enters a contest and wins "A Day with Sir Lancelot (the World's Most Perfect Knight)," he is thrilled. But when the big day arrives, his friends have some doubts—especially Erica. Is Erica just jealous or is there something fishy about the World's Most Perfect Knight? The young dragon slayers are determined to find out—whatever it takes!